Spirit Wanderer

Spirit Wanderer

Raphael Okure

Spirit Wanderer
Raphael Okure

Published by:
Peace Evolutions, LLC
Post Office Box 458-51
Glen Echo, MD 20812-0458

Order books from: info@peace-evolutions.com
www.peace-evolutions.com

Copyright © 2007 Raphael Okure

All rights reserved. No part of this book may be reproduced or transmitted in any form or by any means, electronic or mechanical, including photocopying, recording, or by any information storage and retrieval system, without written permission from the author, except for brief quotations for purposes of a book review.

Printed in the United States.

Cover Art by Raphael Okure
Typesetting and Page Layout by Kent Fackenthall, www.thebukitzone.com

Publishers Cataloging-in-Publication
(Provided by Quality Books, Inc.)

> Okure, Raphael.
> Spirit wanderer / Raphael Okure.
> p. cm.
> LCCN 2007937620
> ISBN-13: 978-0-97-53837-7-3
> ISBN-10: 0-97-53837-7-9
>
>   1. Life--Fiction. 2. Future life--Fiction. 3. Soul
> --Fiction. 4. Fantasy fiction.   I. Title.
>
> PS3615.K87S65 2007   813'.6
>   QBI07-600272

LCCN
ISBN 0-9753837-7-9

The characters and events that appear in this book are fictional. Any similarity to actual people or events is purely coincidental

For friends, and for family;
For love, and for life;
For all, and for God,
whatever your concept of this may be.

SECTIONS

The Beginnings : 3

The Journey of Remembrance : 33

Jack : 99

We, The Wanderers : 133

I remember now… the madness of life: the joy, the pain… The truck. All of it is back, but it only just started making sense. My name is…

Pardon me.

My name *was* Jefferson Hurley; you can call me Jeff. I'm dead now, so the name doesn't really matter.

I'm sure you're wondering how I died, or if I'm even really *dead* at all. Well, it took me a while to figure out what dying was, too. I eventually came to realize that how I died was far less important than how I had *lived.* Whether you know it or not, we're all 'dead' in a sense. Life is really like dreaming while you sleep. Ever had one of those dreams that seemed real as Hell?

Hell… that's another story.

But have you ever had one of those dreams that felt *very* real, and ended only when you were wide-awake? I had a dream like that, once; it involved a toy I wanted very badly. In my dream I clung to it, though I knew I wouldn't bring it out with me. Naturally, I awoke the next morning, clutching my sheets.

Life is like that. You can decide when you 'dream,' and then you have a dream that spans anywhere from five to fifty years. But on the other side of that dream is *this*: where I am, and where you're from. Since you don't remember it, you come up with all sorts of colorful expressions like 'death,' 'the other side,' 'the world of shadows'... and that's even *if* you believe there's something outside the life you know. What you don't realize is that returning to this side is when you 'wake up' – an inevitable act.

Now, I'd like you to imagine several people weaving a quilt. Each person contributes a patch of cloth, which tells a little 'story.' When combined, these patches create the quilt.

It is much the same with us. The stories we tell – the patches we create – are the lives we live, and the lessons we learn in them. We combine these stories to create a tale that is as exciting as it is mystifying, because no one knows what to expect. I suppose you could call us 'Dream weavers.' We each create the details in the grand artwork that is our Universe.

On Earth, you should be especially careful what you weave. When you sleep and have a bad dream there, it disappears when you awake. However, you are still 'dreaming' your entire life there, and as dreams go, yours can be filled with nightmares. When you 'wake up' by returning *here*, you can recreate your entire nightmare. What's worse is, it could take you many years, not minutes, to recover from it. I didn't know this when I returned. In fact, I was quite terrified when I first woke up.

This is my story – or at least, the most important bits. Forgive me if my thoughts wander off on occasion; there is much to be said.

The Beginnings

The Beginnings

1

At some point in life, humans reluctantly face the fact that they will die. For most of them, this is a scary thought. Death is completely enshrouded in mystery, because those who die don't usually come back to tell what it's like.

Due to their inability to comprehend the incomprehensible, some humans compensate by (subconsciously) programming their minds to equate death with pain. This is because pain is a familiar, recurring experience within life, while death isn't. In therefore equating death with pain, many fear death and do everything possible to stay away from it. Problem is, they don't know when or how they're going to die. So they rationalize again, and start 'preparing' around the fourth or fifth decade of their existence, confident in the hand-me-down fact that they are past the "middle point" of their journey, and are now headed down the final stretch.

The question, then, is this: how about the kids who die before they hit twenty-one? Or *ten*? If they had known of their impending departure, they too might have begun making preparations. Your society would classify their behavior as odd. These young ones would be told they are 'too young to die' – with the terms 'young' and 'old' referencing one's relative proximity to birth or death – and they would probably be filled with prescriptions to correct their behavior. In the case of the hypothetical twenty-one year-old, it would mean that s/he was "old" by the time they hit twelve, wouldn't it?

Again, I knew nothing about this – *any* of this – and didn't really care, either. My life was spent blissfully oblivious to such things, and thoroughly enjoyed. I had my own apartment, and was surrounded by three excellent friends with whom I engaged in everything from intellectual conversations to "Friday Night Beer," an activity which involved watching a movie with pizza and, of course, beer.

What about spirituality? Well, none of us – by which I refer to my friends and myself – possessed any more spirituality than a desert has lush vegetation. I could tell you a bit about my companions, to illustrate the point.

Jeremy was older than either Davis, Axel, or myself. Already in his forty-fourth year of life, he was sometimes a father figure to us, and the best custodian you ever met in *any* College. His fascination with video games stemmed from the first electronic games, and continued unabated with more sophisticated modern versions. His experiences with religion were hidden in a past he never really cared to disclose.

Davis, the dreamer, had the good fortune of being raised without religion. Although we would laugh at his occasional 'New Age meanderings,' as we termed them, he did not ascribe to any actual belief system.

Finally, there was Axel, the most practical of us. He was one of those guys who appeared brilliant, but unwilling to pursue their talents. His disdain for religion began when, as a teenager, his father had refused to get his mother to a hospital, convinced that 'a miracle was on the way.' His mother's ailment was in its final stages by the time she *had* arrived at a hospital, and she died shortly afterwards.

In later years, Axel learned that his father had really procrastinated because he wasn't able to afford the treatment anyway. Regardless of this, Axel had retained some resentment towards religion, which he blamed entirely for his father's 'blindness.'

Notwithstanding our differences, we bonded well: four of the best stereotypes that Earth had to offer. Together we avoided anything that required blind faith – from political elections to theology – and the only religion we knew was the one we'd instituted ourselves, which involved Friday nights, beer, movies and pizza.

Forgive my spiel. You're still wondering what happened to me, aren't you? I'll get to that for you.

The Beginnings

2

A drunk driver hit me as I crossed a street, and I eventually died from my injuries. To prevent you from cursing or judging the driver that hit me, I must admit that I was quite tipsy on the night in question. Although I was on foot, I was still responsible for my safety.

I have no regrets about that night, now. You won't either, when I have explained the intricacies involved.

Friday Night Beer was at Jeremy's place. Like most informal traditions on Earth, our activity had evolved a simple schedule that went like this:

I would go to Jeremy's on Friday evening, and we would commence the sacred task of refrigerating the night's primary supply of beer. If this were accomplished ahead of schedule, we would play a video game for about half an hour, while waiting for the other guests.

Davis appeared shortly afterwards, usually with an offering of more beer: the night's secondary supply. What made his special was the fact that Davis was a bit of a dreamer. He would buy the best brand of beer he could find – and sometimes, a pack of fine cigars as well, if he could afford it.

About ten or fifteen minutes after this, Axel would arrive with several boxes of pizza and the night's movies. At this point, 'Friday

Night Beer' would officially begin, solemnly announced by whoever called it first.

That night was to be my last Friday Night Beer for a while. I was moving to a new town, and wouldn't see my friends until I got organized enough to return for visits. Since my friends had chosen to modify this event into a bit of a surprise/farewell party, they had invited another guest: Samantha – or *Sam*, as I knew her. She was a lovely girl, and I actually had a crush on her. When I heard she was coming, I anticipated a memorable night – but I was far from prepared for what happened.

Although there were no tearful goodbyes, I was told at least twenty-six horrible things that would happen to me if I didn't visit weekly. Jeremy himself cast about fourteen of those threats, and the rest were split between Davis, Sam, and Axel. Sam added a few more, when we spent some time alone afterwards, as well as the most memorable kiss I'd ever received in my twenty-three years of existence. It was perfect, and I spent the rest of the night as giddy as a schoolboy – a *drinking* schoolboy.

Jeremy lived on the college campus where he worked, which was across the street from my apartment building. Returning home from his place, I had to make my way to the rear gate of the Campus, then out through a tall picket fence and across a small street. This street had a stop sign, which was now an off-white octagon with a half-hearted warning. I usually checked for oncoming traffic before I crossed. However, on this night I was both tipsy *and* elated (because of the kiss), and my safety was easily forgotten. I felt untouchable!

That was when the truck hit me.

I crashed against the truck's hood, and then to the ground as the driver slammed on his brakes. What I saw next was a fraternity license plate uncomfortably close to my face. Upon viewing the Greek letters on the license plate, I weakly attempted to unravel the last few seconds. My attempt was interrupted by a loud sacred expletive – something to the effect of "*Holy sh…!*"

And then the lights went out.

3

I had an older sister in Delaware. Besides our grandparents – who also lived in another state – she was the only living relative I had. Her job required her to travel frequently, which normally made her impossible to reach. As a result, I often listed Jeremy as my next-of-kin on my official documentation. This was both an affectionate and a practical step, since he would be much easier to reach in an emergency. This proved useful, because the next time I regained consciousness, both he and Axel stood by me. I was in a hospital bed with a forest of IV tubes attached to my body, and I couldn't feel a thing.

As I observed my friends, I discovered I had developed a form of ESP: I was able to 'hear' their thoughts. This was unimaginably depressing: Jeremy was repeatedly blaming himself for letting me walk home alone, and Axel kept wondering if I was going to die. Their grief rapidly overwhelmed my senses.

"You guys need to cheer up," I whispered.

"When you get better," Axel replied, holding back tears. I couldn't explain that I actually *needed* them to cheer up so that I wouldn't feel their grief anymore, so I searched for something else to say.

"I guess I'll have to cancel my trip," I said.

"Yeah," Axel sighed, and brushed away a tear.

"And that means," I continued, "I'll be over on Friday."

This lightened the mood. Jeremy retracted his threats from earlier, since I obviously wouldn't be going anywhere for a while. He did, however, institute a few new ones if I didn't heal before Friday. Axel attempted to do the same, but couldn't bring himself to it. I decided not to disclose my new 'ability,' just yet; I would tell them when I recovered.

Later, when they left, I heard Axel think, "*Man, I hope he doesn't die...*" This worried me; do you remember when I said that I wasn't spiritual? That may have been an understatement. I had been force-fed religion through most of my childhood, and I had been repulsed by it throughout the rest of my life. However, currently faced with the possibility of dying, spirituality returned with a vengeance. Axel's thought lingered in the room, haunting me, and I prayed more feverishly that night than I had my entire life.

It was early morning now. Pain trickled into my tortured consciousness, as I regained a little feeling in my body. The pain soon overwhelmed me, but while I despaired, I started hearing *voices*. I gradually became aware that the silent hallway was alive with activity. A number of people were wandering about or engaging each other in conversation. This was odd; it was always quiet here, at this time of night. Obviously, it was far too late for these people to be visitors... so who were they?

One of them approached my bedside. Her name was Sarah, and she was the mother of two young children. I somehow knew this immediately. I later discovered that my 'ability' allowed me to read memories around people, giving me everything I needed to know from the moment I saw them.

"What happened?" Sarah asked.

"Truck," I whispered.

Sarah nodded sympathetically. She wasn't grieving, like my friends. From her, I felt a maternal, nurturing concern that wrapped around me like a hug. I now *really* hoped my 'abilities' would remain after I healed, because this was *awesome*!

"This may seem a little unusual," Sarah said, "But are you trapped here too?"

I was confused, until my pain blotted her out. I turned away, hoping she would leave. It was difficult to concentrate when my whole body felt like it was being crushed by a whale. For a moment, the pain subsided and I heard her voice again.

"... And I know I should be home, with my kids," she was saying, "but I swear something is *keeping* me here..."

The Beginnings

I turned to her again. What was she talking about?

"I'm telling you," she whispered tearfully, "Something *weird* is going on! I tried to leave, but *I can't get to the door!* I keep winding up in this *same* room." She described what sounded like a hospital room. My mind wandered and, looking behind her, I noticed that the hallway was now almost empty.

I wondered if Sarah was suffering from amnesia or some sort of multiple personality disorder. I didn't understand the bit about her inability to leave the hospital, but didn't want to think on that either. I was about to turn away again when I heard two people hurrying past. As I glanced at each, I *knew* they were nurses, on their way to check on Sarah because something was wrong.

Sarah bolted after them, trying to get their attention. As the noise receded down the hallway, I realized that the nurses had not noticed her.

On subsequent occasions, I learned that most of the others who wandered the hallway were also utterly confused. Eventually, I dismissed them as drug-induced hallucinations, concluding that I may have just been remembering people from the hallway during the day. I would have been content with this conclusion, save the fact that two nights later, I had another visitor. This time, it was a male.

"*Man*," he gasped, "What happened to *you*?"

I began to wonder just how bad I looked.

"*Truck*," I whispered.

"That's messed up, man," he responded, absentmindedly patting his pockets for a pack of cigarettes. When he couldn't find any, he shrugged. He didn't seem to care that it wouldn't have been appropriate to smoke anyway.

"I need to quit," he grinned at me. "Just not on *everything*. The name's Russell."

"Jeff," I introduced myself. Like Sarah, I'd known about him from the moment I saw him. I knew he was here because he attempted suicide, but I didn't proffer any of that.

"I should have really thought about my kids," Russell said, ignoring my introduction. "You know, Corey's gonna be seven on Friday. Jessica's almost nine... let me show you." Excited now, he dug into his jacket again and pulled out a wallet. He held it open before me.

"Aren't they adorable?" he asked.

Having no choice, I forced my attention to the object. I would have gasped at what I saw if I had the strength, because the 'pictures' he was showing me were his *memories* projected into the wallet. I wondered if this was another unexplored part of my new 'ability' and not a hallucination: there was *no way* that I could create something this intricate.

The pain in my body seeped through again, and I closed my eyes. Aware that I was in a lot of pain, Russell decided to take his leave.

"Oh, man... I'm..." he mumbled, by way of apology. "I uh... I'd better... I hope you get better, huh?"

He turned away, and as an afterthought, I heard him add, "I hope *I* get better."

I thought, "Why? He looks fine to me..."

Somehow, he heard me, and stopped to look at his wrists. I heard him let out a scream and, as I watched, he vanished. I never saw him again.

God, I thought, *if you're listening, get me out of here*!

The Beginnings

The following evening, I found myself conscious again. Quickly bored by watching my vital signs, I slipped into one of several alternate realities I'd recently created – this one involving Sam. I thought of her as an extra reason to live. She filled my thoughts as frequently as I was conscious, because I had (optimistically) rationalized that I now had a chance to date her.

As I daydreamed, I was surprised to note that I was focusing a bit *too* intently on her. I was further startled by a loud crackling sound, and I found myself standing right by Sam's bed.

"*Whoa…*" I mouthed slowly. By the vivid quality of my surroundings, I could tell this wasn't a daydream. My mind immediately hunted down a rational explanation.

Of course, my physical condition – and the fact that I didn't know where she lived – made it impossible for me to have journeyed to Sam's room. So, I thought, maybe the brain was capable of abilities like remote viewing, when exposed to a traumatic event. The problem was that this didn't feel like I was *viewing* the room. I had a feeling that I was *there*, by her bed.

I dropped the 'remote viewing' idea and considered lucid dreaming instead. Since, I'd never even been to Sam's, I concluded that my surroundings must have been patched together from my subconscious expectations and combined with her sleeping form to create this experience.

This sounded vague enough to be plausible, and I decided to explore my surroundings, hoping I could get some 'evidence' to investigate later. Just then, Sam stirred in her sleep.

I reflected on how beautiful she looked, and then realized she probably didn't know I was in the hospital. Saddened by this, I wondered what she would think when she found out. I saw her face turn in my direction, and noticed that her eyes were open.

She was staring right *at* me – or rather, where I was standing.

Frantic again, I hoped that I really *wasn't* in her room at that moment, and almost panicked when she sat up. But then, she and her surroundings suddenly vanished, and I was left standing on the roof of her building. I 'knew' it was the roof of her building in the same way that I'd 'known' it was her room.

"Okay," I breathed, "*Weird*."

This *had* to be a dream, my ever-efficient rational mind proposed. Despite its lucid quality, this experience still had the chaotic characteristics of a dream. What then, was the significance of my presence on this roof?

Looking around, I realized I knew this part of town. While it was possible, I wasn't sure this was where Sam lived. I made a mental note to find out from Jeremy or Axel. But would I be conscious enough to communicate my questions? I didn't know – but there was no time to wonder. My surroundings morphed again, and this time I found myself in the hospital room. The various devices that monitored my signals were in clear sight, and with some alarm, I discovered that the device that monitored my heart was now displaying a flat line. Outside the door, footsteps were hurrying down the bustling hallway again.

I considered the possibility that something was wrong with my body. Perhaps this elaborate dream was the brain's way of alerting me to the problem. As I wondered about the approaching figures, I involuntarily found myself scrutinizing them. When I heard one of them think, "*Hold on, Jefferson!*" I experienced a jolt of fear that startled me awake. Pain tore through me again and I roared – but the sound changed pitch when the nurses opened the door. They were the *same people* I'd seen in the hallway.

How did this all relate to everything else I'd seen? There were only two visible differences: I was still strapped to the bed and my pulse was far more exciting than a flat line.

The Beginnings

At the time, of course, I didn't think of my experience as dying, since I had subsequently returned to consciousness – albeit screaming. I wrote it off as a lucid dream. But the more I thought about it, the more it worried me. I mean, I had *seen* the nurses. How could I have observed them without actually leaving my bed?

My rationale soon asserted that I had neither died nor gained precognitive abilities. It proposed instead that my brain had combined the approaching footsteps, memories of the hallway and the sight of the nurses (when they walked in) to effectively render a 'precognitive' or, for some, 'out-of-body' experience.

What seemed like several mornings later, I was conscious again. I turned towards the hallway in time to see a Catholic priest walk by. We made eye contact, and he stopped to proffer comfort or prayers. I could feel his warm, genuine concern, much like Sarah's. Remembering my childhood days, I felt guilty. Why hadn't I maintained my spirituality? Perhaps then, my prayers would have been treated like priority mail, and I would have been out of there, quick as a flash. Or I might not even be here at all. I was, after all, drunk on the night of my accident.

Old memories of sin and sinners returned, and my guilt soon mutated into hatred. I recalled that I'd come to detest religion because I constantly felt inadequate and that I had despised anything that represented religion in any form. Still, I was slipping into that same feeling of inadequacy, as I wondered if so many people in the world with seemingly genuine (and some *verifiable*) experiences could be wrong. I mean, even my own experiences indicated that there was more to existence than the body or brain as a machine…

My attention returned to the priest, and I realized that if the 'many people' were right, it would mean that Heaven and Hell were real. This would also mean that I was making a beeline for Hell, as *nobody* ever really makes it to Heaven – except a few 'chosen ones.' Did I want this priest to reinforce my despair?

"Are you *alright*?" the priest asked me. I attempted to turn away from him, and couldn't. As the world around me slowed down, the sound of my heart monitor was proportionately amplified. I heard the beat slow down, and I saw the priest turn away hurriedly. In one overly dramatic moment, I discovered I was dying: a fact I wasn't ready to make peace with.

Time picked up again, although not soon enough: When the priest returned with a nurse, I was already standing by my body, thinking, "There's *no way* this thing's going to run."

I watched medical personnel rush into the room. Over their shoulders (and the corresponding mental din), I picked out a familiar presence; it was my sister, being restrained from getting any closer. Knowing I couldn't reach her directly, I tried desperately to get back into my body without success. As I began to panic, my rational sense clawed through the scene before me.

This is a dream! It screamed. *The accident never even happened! Just concentrate on getting awake and you'll be fine!*

"But the accident *did* happen," I replied. "I was there: I saw the Greek letters and everything."

No, it was not real! My rational mind responded firmly.

I thought of calling Sàm, to tell her about this crazy dream...

Yes, yes! Call Sam! Call anyone! Just wake up!!

The Beginnings

I woke up on the floor of my apartment, with my face against the carpet. Midday sunlight filtered through the blinds, bringing with it the sounds of an already-active city. I did a double take of my surroundings and heaved a huge sigh of relief, thinking, "That was *definitely* a wild dream."

I was reaching for my phone, which lay on a small table beside me, when I heard the sound of keys outside my door. I froze: only two things could explain an impromptu guest *with keys*. The first was that the apartment's supervisor had decided to check something. Knowing he was meticulous about notifying residents beforehand, I realized that my sister – the only other person with a key to my apartment, who should currently be in Germany – was outside. If she was here… then…

The door opened, and for a moment, I saw my sister freeze. I fell over in surprise and went right *through* the small table. When I looked up, it was clear that she *couldn't* see me. The events of the night before – at the hospital – returned with a rush.

Oh God, I thought, *I'm dead! Dead!*

How could this be? I waited for my rational mind to defend me, but no words came. The world around me began to fade out – *literally*, and not as if I was losing consciousness. My familiar surroundings gradually disappeared, and I was left hovering amidst very distant stars, with my sister's voice occasionally drifting through the void around me. Oddly, I could *feel* she was near, but I couldn't reach her, no matter how much I called out to her.

"Jeff…" I heard her say softly. "Why?"

She started crying. I wanted to reach out and hug her, but then she too – or rather, my connection to her – disappeared.

Resigned to my fate, I thought, "Here it comes. The big *nothing…*"

I anticipated that in a moment, I would be gone too. The few times I'd been bold enough to think about death, I anticipated a complete recycling of my consciousness. Perhaps it would merge somehow with the Universe, and I would cease to exist as an individual form.

But something new filled me: cold dread. Although I still couldn't see a thing, I could tell something was very, *very* wrong.

Before me, a soft glow appeared and rapidly transformed into a bright light. The source of this light, sitting before me, was a *tremendous* Being, and I was under the impression that this was *God*.

…So 'tremendous' may not seem like an appropriate way to describe 'the Almighty,' but you must understand that this being was *huge*. I mean; he was like a mountain of knees topped by a large beard that would have made Santa look bad. I sensed a very stern face behind that beard, and it made me feel weak. And when he spoke? *Man*, that 'mighty waters' thing was *not* a joke.

Was this being 'loving'? Not at all. If anyone I'd encountered over the last twenty-four hours was *'loving,'* it was the priest. This being felt like one of those fathers who would scold you if you cried, and never praise you if you did well. However, his sacred, dictatorial expression was the least of my concerns: What he said next was far more disturbing.

"Now," he boomed, "*Who will testify against this one?*"

The Beginnings

6

Apparently, religion – in its myriad forms – was right. I was about to be judged, and held accountable for everything I'd ever done. I instantly knew this was going to be an unfair judgment, because the only thing I remembered about religion was that one was never good enough.

You know, as a child, I wet myself slightly whenever I got scared. In later years, I learned that the body secreted waste products at the moment of death, and I wondered then if the body 'died a little death' every time I'd thusly wet myself. Thinking back on those times, I concluded that it would be better to have my grandfather screaming at my incompetence than this moment, unable to urinate, and about to face the joys of Heaven or the torments of *Hell*.

Two blurry figures walked out of the void around me. I felt that I *knew* them somehow, but I *really* didn't like them.
"We will testify," they chorused.
"Then let it begin," the Tremendous Being replied. In the ensuing silence, I was abruptly thrust into every memory of my previous existence. No moment was left hidden; when it was over, I felt a little violated.
"Who will testify first?" the Tremendous One asked again. One of the two figures stepped forward.
"I will testify, Majesty," this figure said, "For the wickedness he

has committed."

When waved on, he immediately delved into every petty nuance I had indulged in, even naming such ridiculous things as "Taking money from a coin jar without asking permission." I had an urge to interrupt with a volley of expletives and a more honest account of my life – but I knew that such an outburst could quicken my all-expense-paid trip to Hell. I held my peace… what little of it there was. When the first figure was done, the Tremendous Being nodded in approval.

"Is there *another* who wishes to testify against him?" he boomed as the first figure stepped back. I wondered if it was a formality because the second figure was plainly visible. When he – the second – stepped forward, I got the impression that he was both weaker and infinitely more irritating than the first.

"I will testify for his good, Majesty," he stated, and cleared his throat. The Tremendous One nodded again, and the second being attempted to counter every one of the first being's accusations with the 'good' I had done on Earth, but his speech was useless: Imagine countering a murder accusation with, "While it's *clear*, your honor, that my client murdered the victim, we have evidence that he bought some cookies from a Girl Scout, approximately thirty minutes after the incident. This makes him a good*, innocent* person…"

When he was done, the Tremendous Being grunted in approval again. I felt the watchers around me grow tense. Would they, like the plebeian crowd of the gladiator's heyday, call for mercy or blood? I expected to hear the chant, "*Jugula! Jugula!*" arise at any moment.

"Is there anyone *else* to testify?" the Tremendous One boomed again, clearly for the last time. I knew the call excluded me. I would have been surprised if anyone else stepped forward.

"I have heard the accounts," he announced, addressing me directly. "I have seen your actions. You failed, and are to be…"

I never heard my full sentence: the ground below me was ripped apart, and I was suddenly falling into a large lake of lava below. I saw many others, also screaming in pain, and doing their best to get out of the lava. Ahead of them, on the shore, there was every imaginable and unimaginable form of torture going on.

Far above me, the Tremendous Voice boomed on. The last thing I heard it say was, "Is there anyone to testify against *this* one?"

Then it too was gone.

The Beginnings

Do you know what Hell is?

I hope you never truly find out. I was there – well, one version of it, anyway – and it's *horrible*. It's so bad that none of the scariest movies even comes close to capturing the terror. To give you a better idea, look at it this way; there are fears that your mind *keeps away* from you. There are things you are so scared of that they are buried in your subconscious. If they ever came to light, they could shred your sanity in an instant. These are things you couldn't think of, if someone asked you about your worst fear.

Everything you see in Hell is built from those things. You find yourself frightened by their unfamiliarity, in addition to the fact that they *hurt* you... and this was my sentence for stealing coins out of my grandmother's coin jar.

There was a group of creatures here that saw to the chaos and madness. They instituted acts of cruelty that put some of Earth's killers to shame, ensuring that everyone felt right at home. On occasion, they would kick me in the face[1*] and jeer. It didn't immediately occur to me that they weren't *actually* hurting me as

---

[1*] I should explain that while the floor was intolerably hot, it also had a powerful gravitational pull. It wasn't uncommon to be found prostrate and screaming: Any fantasy of running and hiding from the creatures was immediately quelled.

much as those around me. When I realized it, I wondered if one's measure of punishment was equal to the harshness of their actions. I brushed it aside, though; Hell appeared to be the grand high temple of jails. According to pop culture, the untouched people here should be those who really knew the system: the big-time offenders.

But *I* wasn't a big time offender, and I wasn't really being tortured. As far as I knew, I had been good on Earth: never did anything evil in my life. Why would I get any special treatment here? Perhaps it was a sign that there was some sort of 'repentance' available! Hadn't someone told me, 'No one is ever lost'?

Hopeful that my case could be appealed, I immediately undertook the deepest soul search in my entire – previous – life. I desperately searched through my memories, convinced that there was something to redeem me within. After all, wasn't God 'merciful and loving'?

First place to begin, I thought, was the Ten Commandments – as I remembered them. If I could effectively show that I hadn't broken any of the Big Ten, perhaps I would have a chance to escape this awful place.

For the first commandment, I'd certainly never called anything 'God' besides the 'God' I'd been taught to fear. I admitted that I later hadn't really believed in that same God – but I did again, and clearly he was 'The One;' there was no question about it. I was sure he would see it my way; I moved on to the second.

For the second commandment, I'd never used 'God' as a curse or swear word. I'd learned more colorful expletives, which I had found infinitely more useful in getting the point across.

For the third, I guess I'd never done anything on Sundays – which I'd been taught was the Sabbath, although I later heard that it *wasn't*. This didn't matter; I had always ensured that my Saturdays and Sundays were restful days. Wouldn't I get some credit for taking the trouble? I hoped so again. Again, I convinced myself that if God were merciful, he would see things my way.

For the fourth, well, my parents were long dead. I'd honored my *grandparents*, though. In fact, I was scared to death of grandpa.

For the fifth: *Thou shalt not kill*. Couldn't even kill a bug, because I was so scared of them. The only things I probably ever killed were microbes, and you can blame *that* on the disinfectant and the company producing it.

I moved on to the sixth commandment. Technically, I'd never committed adultery, as I'd neither been married nor with a married

The Beginnings

woman. Fornication – interpreted to me as premarital sex – wasn't in the Top Ten. Hoping to get off on a technicality here, I shakily moved on to the seventh, the eighth... and so on. When it was all done, I imagined my arguments going up to the heights as a glowing ball. For a moment, I saw a small speck of light wink at me from far above. I waited tensely below for a response, convinced that the skies would explode with wings and 'Hallelujahs,' and the same booming voice (which I was now terrified of) would announce that I was forgiven.

No response came. The only thing that happened was that some disgusting creature came by and bit my ankle.

I began to cry. This attracted several of the creatures, and they dropped by to literally shove me around. They would inadvertently claw me in the process; coupled with the immense gravity and intolerable heat, I grew angry.

"*Leave me alone!*" I screamed at them.

"Why are you here?" one of the creatures rasped. The shoving continued, like a game.

"I don't know!" I shot back, feebly resisting them.

"You know what you *diiiid*," they chorused awkwardly, now shoving me in rhythm.

"*Stop!*" I demanded, "*Leave me alone!*"

The cheeky bastards wouldn't listen, and the shoving got more violent. One creature produced a rod and hit me over the head with it several times. As I hit the floor and felt my skin sizzle, I longed again for my hospital bed. The creatures now walked off, muttering something about having taught me a lesson. When I looked up, one of them was raping a woman who was hanging by her hair.

The carnage around me continued: I don't know how much time passed. I looked at my hands, which sizzled as they supported me on the hot floor; the pain didn't matter anymore. When the creature hit me, my head had been cut open, and even now, a steady trickle was maintaining its course down my left temple and onto the floor below, where it burned up instantly.

Why did I have any blood? Didn't it belong to certain organic life forms? I remembered seeing my biological body on Earth; it wasn't the same as what I was now. I mean, I looked and felt the same, but somehow more exuberant.

I rose to my feet and re-examined my hands, which healed as I watched. Everything around me was slowing down again. For the second time since I died, I felt hope again... and *power.* There was no reason to be there, and I knew I was strong enough to rip the place apart if I had to. Around me, the madness had stopped. Most people here were either lounging around torture devices or floating calmly in the lava. It felt like break time. Even the heat was gone; I was no longer afraid.

It occurred to me that I could now 'wish' myself away from this place, like I'd done in Sam's room. I decided to try it out, when some of the creatures returned. I considered destroying them, but knew a fight would be useless since they were also 'energy forms,' like myself. You can't *destroy* energy.

But what was I to do? They were doing *everything* to get to me, now. I calmly wondered where I would want to go. If there had been a Hell, perhaps there was also a Heaven. I resolved to investigate. At that moment, the creatures bounded at me.

"Back the *fuck* off!" I swore. My surroundings disintegrated, as though blown away by a powerful explosion. In an instant, the Hell I knew had disappeared.

When the lights and fragments vanished, I found myself hovering high above the planet Earth.

"Wait," I said aloud, "This can't be right."

The Beginnings

9

Have you ever just stared at the Earth? I'm sure you have, countless times before; maybe you've only forgotten. I haven't forgotten, but then again, I was staring at it a moment ago. It's a moving experience: I recalled an amusing bumper sticker I'd seen, which read, "*Beautiful planet you've got there. Shame, if something happened to it…*"

If you're as skeptical as I was, you might be wondering how I can 'see' anything when I don't have a body. What I call 'seeing' involves picking up *energy waves* or *signatures*. Think of it as a song, with each object or entity as an instrument. Multiple waves create harmonies that you can interact with as a whole, like multiple instruments forming a 'chorus'. This makes things infinitely more vivid because you can clearly observe each object while simultaneously tuned in to the presence of *everything* around you – including the entire *Planet*.

These days, when I visit Earth, I usually pick a position where I can see the mighty Milky Way churning in the background. In those first few moments however, Earth alone captured my attention. All over it, I could see interactions between all forms of life. There appeared to be an unequal distribution of harmony and discord. My attention gradually wandered to the discord alone, and I watched various acts of violence creating 'ripples' over the planet itself.

"Why?" I wondered.

"Because beauty can be disorienting to the untrained mind," someone replied. "The beauty of this one possesses the ones upon her. Now, they destroy her."

I realized I wasn't alone in this place. In fact, there was a massive crowd hovering around me. This time, I was *sure* I hadn't made them up.

"She will survive," someone else said, "But her children may not, if they continue this way. It has always been so."

I admired the galaxy that spiraled in the background. Moments later, I realized the second being had been peering intently at me.

"*You* were in the dream too," she said, still peering. "You appear to have forgotten much."

"Forgotten... what?" I asked. The first being chuckled, and showed me an image of a person staring at the sun. For a moment, I remembered how this temporarily blinded you; still, I didn't see what that had to do with anything. The female being pointed at the sun.

"Do you remember your dream?" She asked. I understood she was referring to my life on Earth.

"This star was always there, woven for this entire system," she continued. "Even now, it remains there, for your use. Has it served you well?"

"I'm sure it has, but what does this have to do with..." I began.

"Now, your star served you with light," she continued, ignoring me, "Whether for growing your plants, or finding your way. Wouldn't it hide itself from you, if you stared at it?"

"Of course not," I shrugged. "But staring at the sun..."

"It is *unwise*, not stupid," she interrupted my sentence. "Every action has its justification either in the eyes of the doer, or the victim. Now, if you were to stare at your star for too long, you could harm your sight. Is this not true?"

I agreed wordlessly.

"But this is not the star's use," she said. "So it is that you may choose to either find your way around with its light, or you may choose to sit and stare at it, blinding yourself in the process."

She turned back to look at the Earth.

"As with your star, so is the dream," she concluded. "Whether or not you treat it as reality, the consequences are yours to bear."

I didn't understand.

"You will, in time," the first being said reassuringly.

10

I didn't *feel* like I had forgotten anything. I decided to ignore this for some time, since the presence of these beings was far more remarkable at the moment.

From my observation, most of them appeared to be casual spectators. Some were actively debating the philosophy of human existence. Several others appeared to be compiling reports. Curious, I turned to the female being.

"What are these people doing here?" I asked.

"Some are here to observe," she replied. "Others are here for other ties."

"Other ties?" I pressed.

"You could call them 'friendships,'" she replied. "Bonds that form and last for generations. They guide each other when it is needed."

This confirmed my observation – albeit at a price. I remembered something about 'spirit guides,' and my skepticism returned with a vengeance.

"See for yourself," she laughed, "*Jefferson*."

She treated the name like a bad word. I was surprised she knew my name, but I remembered my 'ability' back at the hospital, and reasoned that she must have that too.

"There is nothing hidden out here," she told me, apparently confirming my thoughts.

"What's your name?" I asked.

"I don't have one," she replied. "But *you* do, because you carry it with you."

I was about to protest when I realized that I did, in fact, still *feel* like Jefferson Hurley – although Jefferson Hurley was technically *dead*. I was confused again; being dead was turning out to be more complicated than I'd thought.

There was a slight stirring in the group. One of the beings dropped to the surface of Earth, interacted with a child and returned to the vantage point. Several of us watched as the child told its mother that it had just 'spoken to daddy.' She burst into tears at the news.

"In time, she will understand," said the being, apparently the woman's deceased husband. "For now, she believes that such a loss is improper and should be mourned."

Several of the 'stranger' beings seemed to nod in understanding. Some 'recorded' this information.

I wondered why my parents hadn't appeared to take me away, then reasoned that it was probably because I had neither believed in, nor expected it. Then I thought of Jeremy, Davis, and Axel, and wondered how they were coping with my passing. As I thought of each, I found myself observing them – in high-definition detail – *simultaneously*. Not used to this, I whisked myself back to the 'vantage point,' as I'd dubbed it. The female being turned to me. She instantly 'knew' what had just happened to me.

"You should take the time to heal," she suggested, projecting the image of a large city to me. "This place…"

I thought immediately of my 'Hell' experience, and shook my head. She didn't question my decision, and turned back to look at the Earth.

"What happens if I *don't* go?" I asked.

"Oh, you still heal," she shrugged. "But it could take longer."

"Worst case scenario?" I probed further.

"You find yourself trapped in the same place," she replied, referring to my 'Hell.'

"You don't get *sent* back there," she hastily added. "You are free to go about as you please."

I thought of seeing my sister and friends again, but the female being immediately caused me to relive a memory. It was the morning after I died – or to be precise, the exact moment when my sister opened the door to my apartment. I could review the moment in detail, and this time I clearly saw a look of terror on my sister's face.

I realized that she was probably not ready at all to see me and, the more I thought on it, I wasn't ready to see any of my friends either.

"You must be careful with your past ties," the being said. "You are still in a vulnerable state – as are they."

Dispirited, I nodded and turned away from the Earth. I reluctantly allowed myself to sail on, wondering what surprises the rest of Universe held. Maybe I would explore another solar system…

The Journey of Remembrance

1

Innumerable points of light surrounded me, each one a galaxy or star. I thought of one argument against the existence of extraterrestrial *intelligence*, which went like this: notwithstanding the conditions that other creatures might have evolved in, could they have developed belief systems or societies like Earth? Observing the vastness of space around me, I found it difficult to maintain an Earth-centered point of view. To calm myself, I settled with the thought that new life forms wouldn't classify as extraterrestrial intelligence until they fulfilled a few rigorous conditions that I personally set.

A moment later, I encountered another being in what I had thought was an absolutely random path. My movement stopped, and not of my accord.

"I'm sorry…" I apologized, thinking I'd 'bumped' into him.

"And I'm Jack," the figure before me grinned. "Pleased to meet you." He shook my hand, and subsequently opened an umbrella.

"So I hear you just left the Jewel, huh?" he said. The umbrella disappeared.

"The *Jewel*?" I repeated. It was the first time I'd heard the phrase. For brief a moment, Jack appeared confused.

"*Earth*," he said.

"Yes… I guess I *died*…?" I replied, unsure of what to make of this whole 'death' thing. Thus far, everything I'd encountered bore the characteristics of a bizarre dream.

"*Hmm,*" Jack mused. "I see your problem."

"I didn't say I had a problem," I replied.

"Humans don't usually *say* they have a problem," Jack said. "But they usually do. Half the time, they expect you to guess. It's really annoying. So, you weren't *always* dead?"

"I don't suppose I..." I began.

"Yes," he interrupted again. "And you want to go *back*?"

"I didn't say I... you can send me *back*?" I gasped.

He was right: a part of me *still* believed this was a dream.

"I can't help you go back," Jack said. "No one really can, because no one wants to go back. You want to go *that* way."

He pointed at a distant object, but I didn't look where he indicated; I had privately decided to never go anywhere unless I'd heard of it before.

"What if I don't want to go there?" I asked Jack.

"Well, then you won't go," he replied. "But you *do* want to go, because you're here now. Besides, you wanted directions, didn't you?"

"I *didn't* want directions," I countered. "You just gave them to me."

"My apologies," he bowed. "Where were you going?"

"To the..." I began, before I remembered that I didn't actually have anywhere to go. Jack shook his head.

"Humans," he chuckled.

"If you're not human," I queried, "What are you?"

"Complicated," he grinned.

"Okay..." I said, "Doesn't bearing a name from Earth make you a native of Earth?" I asked. He spread his arms.

"Then you must mean that this... Universe... originated from Earth as well," he replied. "A name is a name, and right now, names are not important, *Jefferson*. I'm a traveler, like you. Difference is, I know my way around."

"Let me guess," I said, "*Stick with me, and you'll live forever?*"

Jack looked appalled.

"I certainly don't want *your* company," he said. "If you cannot trust yourself, how can I trust *you*?"

"Trust *myself*?" I repeated, incredulously. "I have a harder time trusting you!"

"Precisely what I said," Jack replied confidently. "I know my way around, and I know many people here. I just came to help, and my task is almost done."

"What do you mean, *almost*?" I asked. He put an arm over my shoulder.

"Right now, you need to look over *there*." He pointed in the same direction again, and I now saw an object orbiting a Red star.

"What's it called?" I asked.

"It isn't," Jack replied. "Stop carrying your dream with you. Not *everything* has to have a name."

"But *you* have a name," I pointed out.

"Only because *you* have one, and I couldn't view you without knowing it," he replied. "*You* don't use your name as an identity; you treat it like a shield! Everyone has to get past it in order to meet you."

This explained why everyone knew my name. I felt stung.

"Now, I will give you two things for your journey," Jack continued. "First, I will remind you how to travel. Do you remember your experiences at the hospital?"

I nodded, surprised that he knew – and then I remembered the female being back at Earth.

"Good," Jack said. "Your experiences were real. Every place is the same place. You only need to remember it, and you'll be there."

"But how do I *remember* a place I've never been?" I asked.

"That is my second gift," he announced. "*Coordinates*!"

He directly transferred information about the slab of rock I was to visit. It had no atmosphere, so it wasn't conducive to biological life. Nevertheless, there was a city built on it, which different from the one I'd been shown earlier. Oddly enough, I also knew *exactly* where the star was located in space.

"Someone's waiting for you," Jack said cheerfully. "See you around!" The umbrella had reappeared in his hand. Raising it, he promptly vanished.

The Journey of Remembrance

When I arrived at the object, I discovered that there were no spectators here. This didn't surprise me: the object before me could hardly be considered a planet. It looked like a gigantic slab of rock, and the large 'spires' sprawled across its unusual landscape appeared to arise from the object itself. Closer observation revealed that some of these were buildings – or might have been, at some point in their existence.

Still apprehensive, I maintained my distance and observed the object in detail. When I decided it was safe, I alighted on the surface. Someone popped up behind me.

"*There you are!*" she screamed excitedly. "I knew you'd get my message!"

I immediately knew this was the person waiting for me.

"Well?" she said. "How did it *go*?"

On Earth, memory loss often came with age. I'd sometimes thought about how awful it must be to completely forget forty percent of a life one worked hard to build. It was a scary prospect – but one I was only peripherally concerned about. Now, it appeared that after I died, a massive case of amnesia was waiting for me.

Thinking on this, I looked again at this female – who seemed very thrilled to see me – and wondered *who* she was.

"You... You've *forgotten!*" she exclaimed in surprise. She peered at me like the other female being had done.

"If you'll excuse me," I sighed, "I've heard that phrase a bit often, since I... got out here, and I *still* don't get it."

"I see," she replied. Unknown to me, she had taken the liberty of thoroughly acquainting herself with my most recent memories.

"You really don't remember who I am?" she asked again. I mumbled apologetically in reply.

"How about now?" she asked. I watched as a change cascaded over her being; soon, she appeared to me as an elderly man with a flowing white beard. She – he – now stepped towards me, smiling. Memories of the Tremendous Being immediately assailed me, and I backed away. I must have been visibly terrified, because the being before me changed into a woman again, this time bedecked in jewels and visibly different from the first female form.

"Who *are* you?" I demanded. She changed into a llama in high heels.

"I'm gorgeous," she croaked. "Who are *you*?"

"Is this entire Universe filled with *Cheshire cats*?" I groaned. "Please *stop* that. It's annoying!"

"Sorry," the being apologized. "Allergies." She sneezed and turned into a potted plant.

"Alright, genie," I said, turning to leave. "I think I'm done here."

"Wait!" she called. Turning to her, I saw she was again using the first form I'd seen.

"What *happened* to you?" She asked.

"I lived, died and went to Hell," I replied. "Then I came *out* of Hell and met a lot of weird people."

"Well, the first thing you need to do is get fixed up," she told me, patting my back. I immediately thought of the city I'd been previously shown, and refused immediately.

"Or... we could just *talk* you out of it," she sighed. "Whatever happens, I will be watching you from now on."

"I'm sure I *do* need whatever help I can get, if things are as bad as people tell me," I said cautiously. "But could you please stop the shape-shifting thing? With what I just went through, I probably won't handle it very well, and if there's any funny business, I'll leave immediately." I imagined retreating to the nondescript point in space where I'd met Jack, reasoning that if this being read my mind, the location would be too ambiguous for her.

"*Right*," she smiled. I sensed that there was nothing more to be done about it.

"Let's hear it, then," I sighed. "What's this thing that I'm supposed to remember? What am I missing?"

"*Me*," she smiled.

"What about you?"

"If you have forgotten *me*," she replied, "Then there's *a lot* you have to remember."

3

After a moment of stunned silence, I managed to repeat, "*You*?"

"What did they *do* to you?" she asked.

"Everyone's been asking the same thing," I told her. "The only thing I can gather from my trip so far is that Earth is pretty messed up, and so am I."

"All will turn out as it should," she said.

"Right," I replied. "Destiny, fate, whatever. Is this the stuff I forgot?"

"What do you *want*?" she sighed. "A news update?"

"That might help," I replied dryly. She immediately assumed the form of a news anchor.

"To-*day*, on Channel Four hundred and seventy-*nine*," she began.

"Stop," I warned.

"*You* stop," she retorted.

"Stop what?"

"Repressing memories," she replied, and changed to her first form.

"You think I'm *deliberately* doing this?" I was getting exasperated.

"Calm yourself," she said. "No one's accusing you of anything. All I'm saying is that you should be careful, or something might sneak up and bite you."

I had a feeling she meant that literally. Quickly looking behind me, I spotted a hideous little creature about to bite my ankle. As I sprung away, it disappeared.

"That was *not* cool!" I screamed at the female before me.

"You're right," she laughed. "But it *was* funny."

"Fine!" I screamed, and turned away again.

"What do you want?" She called out again. "*Pity*? You put that creature behind you! This is not your first time here! Wake up, *Jefferson!* You're not the only 'dead' person around here."

My bruised ego had only heard as far as the word, 'Pity.'

"I *don't* want pity," I shot back. "Some *understanding* would be nice, though, instead of... of crazy magic tricks."

"Then I'll give you understanding," she replied calmly. "Understanding that you put that thing behind you, and understanding that you don't understand that you *did* put that thing behind you, I'll assist you with further understanding yourself, until you understand everything that has just happened here."

I fell silent.

"That's a mouthful," she said, as an afterthought. "But at least, you're not screaming at me anymore."

Realizing I'd been a bit rude, I apologized for my outburst.

"It's *understandable*," she smiled. "Look, I want you to remember things as much as you want to remember them. I'll help in any way I can – and I'll start by addressing you by your last name."

"*Hurley*?" I asked. "That brings back horrible memories from middle school gym class."

"Not *that* one," she said. After a brief pause, she said, "*Jefferson*."

"Ah, that," I said. "Alright; what's *your* name?"

"My last name was *Kufe*," she replied. I thought it sounded rather exotic.

"It is," she replied to my thoughts. "It wasn't from the Jewel."

I wondered at this again. She was as human as Jack. Perhaps it was the feeling of camaraderie each had presented.

"It's a pleasure to meet you," I said, extending my hand.

"It is good to see you again," she replied, and took my hand. For a moment, everything stopped. I felt as though I'd just shared the most complete, Universe-shredding orgasm with her. For the second time since I'd died, I felt violated again – but this time, it felt *good*. She heard my thoughts and laughed. I found her laughter vaguely familiar, like someone from a lost memory – which, according to her, she was.

"Uh… shouldn't I buy you a drink first?" I mumbled, somewhat embarrassed.

"Why?" she asked. "I don't drink. Besides, that's not the first time we've shared that. I'm surprised it didn't spark up any more memories for you."

"What do you mean?" I asked.

"Well, you *enjoyed* it, didn't you?" she asked me.

I assented uncomfortably. "Is that how people greet each other around here?"

"Only if you *really* know each other," she replied, "Or if you really want to. Depends on who starts it."

"Which of those was it for you?" I asked.

"Both," she laughed, and changed into a tree. She immediately changed back with apologies.

"So, apparently, I know you, and you know me," I said to Kufe later. "But I don't remember you at all."

"Well," she said slowly, "It seems that you think this is your beginning."

"Beginning of what?" I asked.

"Of your existence," she informed me. "You think that it all began when… *Jefferson* was born as a child. Since you've forgotten everything before that, you find it very odd that I know you."

"I find it odd that *everyone* I met knew me," I replied.

"Out here," Kufe explained, "You're an open book. *Everyone* you meet will know everything about you from the moment you meet them."

"Great," I groaned.

"What do you have to hide?" she laughed. "That's the way it's always been."

"I know," I sighed, "I don't remember."

"Good," she said. "We're getting somewhere."

"So *everyone* knows my thoughts?" I asked.

"Nothing wrong with that," she replied. "I can understand your caution, but I must remind you, *Jefferson*, that you're not on the Jewel anymore."

She was right. Many would be embarrassed to get their morning coffee if the pretty cashier could hear their thoughts.

"Back to something you said earlier," I told Kufe. "What's this about 'beginnings'?"

"Well," she replied, "We've *always* been together, which is why

I know you. It's also the reason behind the little 'moment' we shared. I'm sure you will remember…"

"Here we go again," I groaned.

"It's true!" she protested. "If I were to rattle your history off to you now, it wouldn't make any sense. However, if you *remembered* it yourself, it would mean more. That's why you have to go to the City. There are ones who can…"

She picked up my unspoken thoughts and stopped.

"You're still concerned about being judged, aren't you?" she asked. I nodded.

"But you've already judged *yourself*," she said. "You think you're unworthy of something, and you're running away from being punished. You are, in *essence* – no pun intended – carrying the very judgment you fear with you, and taking it everywhere you go!"

Again, she was right. The whole 'Tremendous Being' saga had obviously been unreal, so… nothing was going to judge me – right? I groaned aloud.

"You'll recover," Kufe smiled. "Right now, you need a little rest."

"Or a stiff drink," I muttered.

"What *happened* to you?" she chuckled, shaking her head.

4

After my 'rest,' Kufe engaged me in conversation again.
"Tell me what happened," she requested.
"What happened where?" I asked. "When?"
"When you left... *Earth*," she said.

I considered the question, and decided it would be best to tell her how I had died. I recounted what I have already told you, beginning from the night of the accident and ending with the close encounter of the Tremendous Kind. Kufe shook her head when I was done. I was more comfortable with her now, and gave her details about the Tremendous Incident. She laughed hysterically.

"You reviewed your life badly," she said. "But I understand better why you are reluctant to go to the City."

"It's a little odd to find out there's no heaven or Hell," I said. "But nothing else that I believed in turned out to be real; I'm not going anywhere else unless I know where it is. You have to understand that it was hard enough to come *here*."

Kufe nodded.

"So what's to do?" I asked now. "I'm apparently confused, and I'm reluctant to go to this... *City* thing... what is that place called?"

"It isn't," she said. I remembered Jack.

"Who was that... that *Jack* guy?" I probed further.

"You'll meet him later," she replied, smiling. I was about to protest, but she cut me short.

"You have much to remember," she said. "Right now, you don't actually *have* to do anything. When you do, you'll get to decide what it is."

"I have a question," I said. "I spent most of my childhood going to church, right? Then I spent the rest of my life hating the thought of church, and just not caring. Does *any* of that account for anything?"

"I don't understand," she said.

"Well," I began, and paused. "Will I get *punished* for that, for instance?"

"No," she replied simply. I waited for her to continue, but she didn't.

"*No?*" I ventured.

"This is something else you need to deal with," she said. "You think you're in the hands of something or another. You leave your fate to the hands of some large being…"

"No, *no*," I hastily interrupted. "I'm quite sure the size factor was somehow my fault."

"May be," she replied. "But you still believe that it – the being – is responsible for your life and afterlife. At what point will you think for yourself?"

I made no reply.

"It would be a shame," she mused. "What sort of existence would it be, if one existed only for the pleasure of another? Your system is flawed, it seems," she said.

"What system?" I asked.

"The one you were raised into," she replied. "You were taught about good and evil as absolutes. You were also taught to believe that if ever you deviate from what you've been schooled, you would have blasphemed against some Supreme Authority, and therefore deserve punishment for your error."

"That may be," I shrugged, "But I always had a problem with authority. I'm still having trouble believing in a Creator at all."

"Then, I will show you something," Kufe said. She touched my arm. Our surroundings faded out, giving way to innumerable galaxies. We were hovering – or standing – somewhere in space, and the view was all the more breathtaking because there were no beings around.

"Lovely, isn't it?" Kufe said, and touched me again before I could ask any questions. Our surroundings changed, and I again felt the presence of many other beings nearby. Each appeared to be making some sort of music that combined to form a complex and beautiful harmony.

"Who are they?" I asked, entranced.

"Wanderers," Kufe replied. "Some are among the eldest around."

"What are they doing?" I asked again, still watching the symphony of motion.

"Many things," Kufe replied. "Mostly weaving stars."

"They... *stars*?" I repeated.

"Yes, stars," she said.

Eventually she realized I'd been staring at her for some time.

"*What*?" she exclaimed. "See for yourself!"

She was right: There *were* stars being woven here. I could see that it was a painstaking process – even if the collaborating artists appeared to be having lots of fun with it. Still, I refused to believe it.

"So I'm supposed to believe," I said slowly, "That *every* star was *woven*?"

"Believe what you want," she laughed, and touched my arm again. We found ourselves hovering before Earth. It was nighttime over the continental United States. The crowd of watchers was nowhere in sight.

"What do you remember of your time here?" Kufe asked.

"Some of it," I replied, after a brief pause. "Why?"

She touched my hand, and we reappeared on the Pit Stop.

"What do you remember about the origin of life on the Jewel?" Kufe asked me later.

"Why don't you ever say 'Earth'?" I asked.

"Because you gave it that name," she replied. "Remember, nothing really has a name. Now, what do you remember about the origins of life on your *Earth*?"

I was about to boldly launch into the theories of evolution and something about the Big Bang – in *that* order – when I remembered that nothing I'd learned in the course of my existence had proven completely true, thus far. Kufe heard my thoughts.

"This 'Bang,'" she said, "What is it?"

"Just a theory," I replied, hoping to skirt the topic. "I mean, there were many proposed explanations."

"Like what?" she pressed.

"Like…" I paused. "*Many* things. There were cultural myths, for instance, and even crazy theories about genetic manipulation. If it wasn't one thing, it was another."

Kufe shook her head.

"No wonder you were confused when you left," she said. "Were you taught about stars?"

"Stars are -" I began, then remembered what I'd seen.

"Stars are… *what*?" Kufe urged.

"…In… the *past*," I said, again trying to avoid a direct answer. "It takes time for light to travel from them to Earth, so what we see

– *saw* – was in the past."

"So," she said slowly, "It was easier for you to look at the past in your night sky than it is to believe that those same stars are being *woven*?"

I remained silent.

"That's the *last* time I let you wander off by yourself," Kufe sighed, shaking her head again.

"Look," I replied, "I'm not saying you're not making any sense – I mean, for *crap's* sake, I saw those guys myself. I'm just wondering where science went wrong."

"Did you listen to *anything* your parents taught you about God?" she smiled.

"My *grandparents*," I corrected, "And no, I didn't."

"Then why listen to your schooling?" she laughed. "Throw it out as well!" She carelessly generated a pinpoint of light in the palm of her hand, and made it shoot off like a tiny comet.

"Make a wish," she told me.

6

"You know, I read a story like this once," I told Kufe.

"What happened in it?" she asked. I was about to reply with something derogatory towards "New Age thought," but decided against it. It was a bit hard to get over the fact that I was *dead*.

"Well, some guy died and learned things from his spirit guide," I told her. "Then he returned to Earth."

"I'm not your spirit guide," Kufe said.

"I didn't think you were," I replied. "Then again, I never really thought they existed."

I remembered the watchers above Earth, and was forced to quietly reconsider my statement.

"I asked you earlier about life on the Jewel," Kufe said. "You told me of the 'proposed explanations' you heard. How many of these were true?"

I was about to propose evolution, when I recalled that it too was a theory – albeit the most scientifically plausible. Then the star weavers came to mind, and I groaned.

"You know," I told Kufe, "I'm not so sure any more."

"Isn't it possible," she ventured, "That *all* of them are true – or at least, hold some truth?"

I thought on the various theories, searching for a common thread.

"Nope," I replied confidently. "They were far too varied to have shared a common origin."

"That's true," she said. "But that could also be because they come from vastly different sources."

I paused, waiting for more. Kufe didn't speak.

"*What?*" I demanded. Satisfied at my curiosity, she gave me a smug look.

"Think about it," she said. I shook my head. There was no way I could reconcile an Egyptian myth, for instance, with the theory of evolution – or even Panspermia.

Kufe sighed.

"You said there were different origins," she said.

"Yes, I did," I agreed. Again, she said nothing more.

"And... that means... *what?*" I asked again.

"You *know* this, Jeff," she said. "Think about it."

I tried, but still couldn't get it. I could only come up with one thing: over millennia, it was possible to confuse a story if it were passed down orally. However, the myths and legends that currently existed were too vastly different from the proven...

This was getting me nowhere, and Kufe knew it.

"Alright," she sighed. "I'll give you a hint. If the people of Earth knew about star weavers, do you think life there would be different?"

"Well, if they found out *now*," I proposed, "They would probably freak out."

"True," she replied, "But that's not what I mean. If they had shared the story of these star weavers for generations, would there be so many theories in existence?"

"Probably not," I said.

"*Exactly*," she clapped. "Or at least, your other theories wouldn't be *absolute* truth. But *you* now know that there *are* beings who weave stars."

"Don't remind me," I groaned.

"But isn't it true," Kufe continued, "That stars are formed by the same forces that your science has proven?"

It was true. Such discoveries paved the way towards the first weapons of mass destruction.

"I suppose you're right..." I said slowly. "I mean, I didn't watch an experiment myself... but I'm pretty sure there's science involved there somewhere."

"*Exactly!*" she cheered again. I still didn't get it.

"I swear," she sighed, noting my bewilderment again. "This is the very last time I let you explore on your own. I've never seen you *this* damaged before."

"And I'm sure I've never seen it either," I snapped. "Look, you just said that *some* stars are born through nuclear fission…"

"And you just agreed that some stars are 'woven,'" she replied.

"So, what?" I queried. "We're *both* right?"

"*Now* he gets it," she said and, throwing up her hands, fell over on her back. I ignored her antics.

"You're saying *all* the creation myths are true?" I gasped.

"Not entirely," she said. "There's one more bit to the puzzle. If you had been told about the star weavers on the Jewel, would you have believed in them?"

"Of course not," I replied.

"And if you had heard that your science wasn't worth anything," she continued, "Would you have believed that too?"

"I probably wouldn't have listened," I sighed, longing for the luxury that was blissful ignorance.

"That's what I mean," Kufe finished. "We would have held two different perspectives, each with proof, but still we would *both* be wrong."

I remembered a poem about six blind men who encountered an elephant. In attempting to describe the elephant, each blind man would feel one specific part of the animal and insist that they had described the whole.

"The stories you heard on *Earth* were varied for a reason," she continued. "Each was based on something real. As you can tell, humans are not very good with preserving memories, even when they're attached to those memories. Do you think every being on that world came from the same place?"

I made no reply; I already knew her answer.

"Well, *everything* that exists came from *one* place," she said. "–but not every being on the Jewel is from there. When you go into such a world, you forget your existence here. Do you remember any of your dreams from there?"

"I've heard the word 'dream' used in different ways," I said, "So pardon me if I'm a little slow with a response."

"On the Jewel, when you rested at night," she explained. "Do you remember any of the things you saw?"

I couldn't remember any dreams – except the one I mentioned much earlier. Even then, I'm sure that wasn't the entire dream; just a part of it.

"In the same way, you will remember bits out here," Kufe said. "Eventually you'll remember all you need. Also, like your life on the

Jewel, you would return to sleep the next night, knowing there was a possibility that you would dream. Isn't this true?"

I nodded.

"Most of your dreams were reflections of your daily life, even if they were usually poor representations," she continued. "Your life itself was a poor representation of your actual existence. Like a dream, it tried to find and reflect its origins. Sometimes, a being will find a reason to live: a goal to strive for. This only becomes a problem when the being treats their goal as absolute truth for *everybody*."

"So is this to suggest," I said, thinking of the Chinese creation legends, "That some people really evolved from massive mosquitoes that once fed on a giant?"

"No," Kufe smiled, "But you can believe that, if you want."

"I still don't completely get it," I said. "So, for every story or theory I've heard, there's an element of truth?"

"Hey, *you* lived there," she said. "Didn't you see it yourself?"

"Have you ever been to Earth?" I queried. "Do you even know anything about Earth?"

"I know plenty about *Earth*," she retorted, "Because we've *both* been there. Let's settle this." She turned away from me.

"Hey, *Jack*!" she called. Jack suddenly appeared by us.

"You rang?" he said.

"Remember the thing in the place?" Kufe said. "Is any of it true?"

"Ancient astronauts?" Jack replied. "*Yeah!*" And with that, he vanished again.

"See?" Kufe said, "I *told* you."

I was far too confused by the entire encounter to reply.

"Now," she continued, "Do you remember the ones that were watching your world?"

"Yeah, but…" I began.

"There are many like that," she interrupted. "Once in a while, they'll have a dream – you know, to get their hands dirty – and other times, they will just watch from a distance. You won't believe how many people were sent *into* the dream by others."

Given the sheer size of the crowd I'd seen, and the size of Earth's overall population, it didn't seem too far-fetched to think that there were probably 'aliens' in existence. However, what Kufe mentioned alluded to reincarnation, which I was still unwilling to consider.

"I can see you're having trouble with this," Kufe said, again picking on my thoughts. I nodded in reply.

"Then I suppose this would be a bad time to tell you that there are other reasons for a star's existence," she said cheerfully.

"Are you about to tell me of some celestial mass-production plant?" I asked. "Or that people live on stars?"

"Something like that," she said.

"People *live* on stars?" I repeated, surprised.

"No," she replied. "Some stars *live*."

I stared at Kufe blankly.

"There is much you have forgotten," she sighed, "And even more that you haven't explored. Did you ever wonder about your existence in the dream?"

"All the time!" I scoffed.

"*All* the time," she repeated disbelievingly.

"Well... yeah, I mean, when I was a kid..."

"What happened afterwards?" she asked.

"I went to school, like all good kids did," I replied. "Tried to make something of my life."

"And did you achieve that?" Kufe pressed.

"I was about to move," I told her. "New town, new possibilities."

"Were you going to reconnect with your childhood?" she asked.

"I'm sure I did," I protested weakly. "At least, intermittently. But you grow up to find that there is no place for childhood curiosity in adult life."

She studied me for a while.

"So you felt there was no reason to," she finally pronounced.

"There wasn't," I replied. "As the saying goes, 'there are more important things in life.'"

"Such as what?" she asked.

"Bills," I replied. "Education. Bills incurred from education. Raising a family. You get the idea."

"And these were more important than the goal of your existence?" she asked again.

"To many," I replied, "There is no ultimate purpose. We're random biological products of evolution in an ultimately chaotic

Universe."

"You believed one thing," Kufe said. "Then you 'died.' When are you going to face that?"

"You know," I said, "It's a little difficult for me to accept that I don't actually have a *face* anymore."

Kufe laughed.

"By the way, *you're* not off the hook," I said, seizing the opportunity to avoid scrutiny. "What's this about *living stars*?"

"Stars, *planets*," she shrugged.

"Planets!" I exclaimed.

"Think," she said deliberately, "Of the *star weavers*. Nothing is impossible here."

I thought instead of ripping out my hair. Kufe sighed.

"That's it," she said. "You're coming with me."

"Where to?" I asked.

"To see several old friends," she replied, and touched my arm.

"Yours?" I asked.

"*Ours*," she replied. The surroundings blurred.

We stood in an unearthly, rocky wilderness. Ages ago, this place must have been alive with rivers of lava or mud, crashing down hills and over cliffs. Now, the enormous lakes and streams lay frozen in time as curious geological formations.

In the distance loomed four mountainous shapes. Closer scrutiny revealed that these shapes were actually *huge* pyramids. To my knowledge, pyramids were products of old civilizations on Earth; what were these large ones doing on a planet that was clearly *not* Earth? I hurried after Kufe, who was now walking in their direction.

"Why didn't we just appear *there*?" I asked her.

"Because you need the exercise," she replied, poking me.

"But I was under the impression that I looked rather splendid," I joked. It wasn't far from the truth; I did *feel* rather splendid.

"Based on your current state," Kufe said, "You're probably going to be very disturbed after we arrive. I wanted you to get it out of your system; to lose some of that weight you're carrying."

"But what's at the pyramids?" I probed.

"You'll see," she replied.

I observed the pyramids again, and remembered Jack's last appearance; "Ancient Astronauts?" he'd said. "*Yeah!*" So, this was another civilization – which meant that there *was* other intelligent life in the Universe. Was this a primitive race, though? It was possible, considering the fact that these pyramids – although huge – seemed to be in better shape than the ones in Egypt. Had the inhabitants of this area never progressed past the Stone Age? But I sensed that these pyramids were also much *older* than the ones in Egypt. Again, I found myself very confused.

Kufe slipped her hand into mine, briefly interrupting my thoughts. I realized that I felt comfortable with her now.

"What's the name of this place?" I asked her.

"There *isn't* one," she sighed, as though she had anticipated the question.

"Oh, *right*," I nodded. I searched for something else to say.

"Pyramids," I finally announced. "Really big ones. Why?"

"Well you…" Kufe began. "Ah… you'll find out soon enough."

"But I…" I began.

"I know," she interrupted. "You thought they were 'invented' on *Earth*. For the last time, the Jewel is *not* the only populated world in existence."

"Besides," someone else said, "They are excellent structures for withstanding quakes. I *knew* I heard you."

I turned to see a male being land beside us: a being, I thought, who looked like a cross between a figure from old Egyptian and Mayan mythology. Large powerful wings adorned his back, and his head looked like that of a bird of prey, complete with a hooked beak. Feathers cascaded down his neck onto a torso that had clearly been sculpted from hard work, and not the gym. I turned to look at the pyramids again, and it began to make sense.

"Oh my God!" I gasped. "Oh… my *God!*"

The avian was confused by my display.

"It is good to see you two again," he said. Turning to Kufe, he asked, "What troubles *him*?"

"It is good to see you too," Kufe replied. Gesturing at me, she said, "*He* was in the Jewel."

"Ah," the avian nodded. "And that would mean… I see."

I should explain here that our communication was also done telepathically – except the nod, of course. I was initially disappointed, as I'd hoped to hear what otherworldly squawks made up his language.

I was soon lost in thought again. If this guy had wings, then he wasn't… well, *dead* like Kufe and I – since he might actually need them to fly. But then again, he was able to see *and* interact with us. *How?*

"It appears he has been very much affected by this," the avian now said, turning to Kufe. "Did you…"

"He refuses to go to the City," Kufe replied, quickly relaying the details of my 'Hell' experience.

"The state of affairs on the Jewel is troubling," he said, when she was finished.

"You know," I spoke up, "Frankly, I'm quite concerned with the... uh... state of affairs on the Earth myself."

Kufe and the avian turned to me, puzzled.

"Seriously," I continued. "Since I left, everyone's been telling me just how bad it is."

"Many have taken their dreams too seriously," the avian told me, "Much like yourself."

"I take it this is not a good thing," I said.

"Well, look at *your* situation," he replied. "You stand here, observing me like a..." He searched my mind for the words, "*Biological anomaly. Yet, if I were to tell you now* that we have shared thousands of your years in friendship, you would not believe me. Yet it is the truth."

"*Thousands* of years?" I repeated slowly. What was he talking about?

"This knowledge is no longer shared on the Jewel?" asked the avian, in response to my thoughts.

"He has refused to go to the City," Kufe said again, "So I have brought him here with the hope that we can restore some of his past to him."

The avian nodded.

"Perhaps," he said, turning to me, "We can start by reminding you of your time *here*."

"Wait, *what*?" I said. "I *lived* here?"

Kufe started laughing. The avian turned and, after a brief exchange with her, started laughing too.

"What's the joke?" I asked, cautious now.

"She just said," the avian replied, "That it would probably be a bad time to tell you that you built one of *these*."

He gestured broadly at the pyramids behind us.

As we walked before the towering structures, I wondered how *I* was involved in bringing them into existence. What were they for? Was there *any* connection between these and the ones in Egypt?

"So many questions," Kufe sighed, reading my thoughts.

"I think you'd be just as confused," I retorted. "Whether or not I know these things – as you claim – right now, I don't remember any of it, so it's all pretty new to me."

"You were one of the first here," the avian said. "You too helped to weave this world."

"I did?" I said.

"He has a little trouble believing that things can be *woven*," Kufe said. "Maybe you should just tell him about the Library."

"What Library?" I asked.

"This one," the avian replied, pointing at the largest pyramid in the group. It stood in the center, and towered over the rest by several feet. I was in awe of its sheer size.

"What's in it?" I eventually managed to ask.

"Many things," the avian said. "We collect information from many places and stored it here."

"That thing looks like it could hold a *lot* of information," I mused. "How much exactly is *in* there?"

"You should know," the avian replied. "You were *just* here."

"He might not remember that," Kufe said.

"How long ago?" I asked.

"About two to three hundred years, by Earth's time," she replied.

"Yeah," I said. "I probably wouldn't remember that. I have trouble remembering anything that happened before I was *seven*."

"Then you are unprepared for anything inside." the avian said.

"Can't I just take a peek?" I begged.

"You would have to unlock it," he told me, "And you don't remember how."

I surveyed the entire surface of the pyramid and found no openings at all. The entire thing looked like it had been carved out of a mountain in one piece.

"At least, tell me how I *store* the information," I sighed, exasperated.

The avian held up his hand, and a ball of light formed in it.

"You store your findings in light," he replied. He had hoped that I would have remembered at that point, but I was meanwhile wondering how many bytes of information could be stored in the ball of light. No matter how I tried, I didn't see how it was possible.

"So, if this thing basically contains my memories, or *memoirs*... whatever you call them," I said, "Why can't I access it?"

"Because you can't unlock it," Kufe said.

I began to protest.

"You locked it, *Jefferson*," she interrupted. "You can open it just as easily."

I looked at the pyramid again, stumped that I could have been involved in the creation of something so massive. Since everything out here didn't have a name, how then did I recognize things? Thinking of Kufe, I realized now that even if I didn't know her by that name, I could still differentiate her from the other beings I had encountered – by somehow just *knowing*. Looking at the nondescript mountain of stone before me, I understood that if I had closed it, I would instinctively know where the door was. I familiarized myself with it again and *voila,* I found the door! Kufe and the avian followed me as I circled the pyramid again. As anticipated, a door stood waiting where there previously hadn't been one. The avian stopped me there.

"I still think you are unprepared," he said. "Now, I could ask *her* to come with me, but you might be uncomfortable with the thought of being left alone – and *I* am uncomfortable with leaving you out here."

"Oh, I'm *not* letting him out of my sight anymore," Kufe reassured him.

"Then I will return shortly," the avian turned to me, "If I have your permission. What do you want to see?"

"I… don't know," I said. The avian perused my thoughts again.

"You have many questions," he mused. "I will see what is most relevant."

With that, he disappeared into the pyramid.

9

"You know," I remarked, "If that guy had visited Earth a few thousand years ago, he might have been immortalized as a god."

"He *is* immortal," she replied. "And that's why he didn't go."

"You mean, he had the opportunity?" I asked.

"You know the story," Kufe smiled. "It's all you've been thinking about since we arrived here."

"The 'ancient astronaut' deal?" I asked.

"That is not what I would call it," she said. "Are *you* an astronaut?"

"No," I replied.

"But you are," she said, "You too have traveled amidst stars."

"We'll come back to this later," I said. "But how can he *see* us?"

"How can't he?" Kufe asked.

"Okay, look" I said, "He actually *uses* his wings, and doesn't just zap around like we do. I've come to understand that you don't have wings unless you need them, which is why I didn't believe in angels. It also probably explains why I haven't seen anything with wings, except him. So – he's *physical*, right?"

"Yes," Kufe agreed, "Like you and I."

"*No*," I sighed, wondering how to express myself. I decided to settle for either a phrase I had previously disdained, or 'dead.' Since I was still uncomfortable with the 'D' word, I settled for the former.

"We're... *energy bodies*, aren't we?"

"*Everything* that exists is energy," Kufe replied. "Energy comes from energy. Space is filled with energy."

"Alright," I conceded. "I'll put it this way, then; if he went to Earth, would people be able to see him?"

"If he *wanted* to be seen," Kufe shrugged. "But based on what you're going currently through, I don't think he'd want that."

"So, some guys went from *here* to Earth?" I asked.

"Not all were from *here*," Kufe replied. "There has been interest in the Jewel for a long time. Many have gone there to attempt to effect change; among them, beings who wove their own bodies. In that time, such a thing was not uncommon: now, you think it is impossible. This is part of the reason you don't see the Elders anymore."

"I think a lot of things are impossible," I replied. Kufe generated another pinpoint of light in her hand and blew it at me like a kiss. At that moment, the avian returned from the pyramid, holding what appeared to be a small, pale-blue ball of light.

There are three memories," he said. "I have arranged them for you." He held out his palm, and I touched the light, which surrounded me. Within it, I found myself in a room, somewhere on Earth. I *knew* it was Earth in the same way I'd known I was in Sam's room. Before me was a gilded table, atop which lay an artfully crafted, bloody knife.

Oddly, I remembered this scene, but as if it was from an old dream. It wasn't from Jefferson's life; it seemed older.

"Remember what you have seen," the avian told me.

The light changed color, and a woman appeared by me. Although it was not immediately obvious, I knew I wasn't on Earth anymore. I now stood in a large room with enormous pillars, and a highly polished floor. I looked down to see my reflection; the face I viewed didn't belong to Jefferson.

"This time was spent in a place that had advanced far beyond the Jewel," the avian explained. "In fact, you had recently hoped to share some of their knowledge with the Jewel, but decided against it shortly after arriving."

"I did?" I said. "Why?"

"You understood that the knowledge wouldn't be used properly," he replied. "So you decided to end your dream differently."

I gestured at the woman beside me. "Who's *she*?"

"Your wife," I heard Kufe reply. "A Keeper of the Records, like yourself."

"What sort of record was kept here?" I asked.

"Nothing exciting," she replied. "You might like to know that this race knew humans a long time ago."

I thought again of the Ancient Astronaut theory.

"Genetic experiments?" I asked.

"No, no," Kufe replied. "I should say they interacted with an older human *civilization*."

"You mean the Old Gods?" I gasped.

"No," the avian said. "It was an earlier and different time."

I was still stumped. I remembered claims about Egypt and the mythical Atlantis possessing more advanced technology than present-day humans on Earth.

"Oh, it's even older than *that*," Kufe assured me.

"I wonder if it wouldn't be best to just seal him in the Library," the avian mused.

"It might help," Kufe agreed.

"Yeah," I added, "What's the worst that could happen?"

"You could rip yourself apart," Kufe said, and turned to the avian. "Why have you shown him this moment?"

"Because of the first memory," the avian replied, and turned to me.

"Look at your companion," he said.

I looked at Kufe, and suddenly felt *relieved* that she was there. It felt as if I had previously lost her, and I was now determined to never let it happen again. I relayed this to the avian.

"This is good," he said. "Now, call on the first memory."

I did, and now experienced the horror and rage that had accompanied the event. I now understood *why* the blade was there, and trembled with rage. Instinctively, I grabbed Kufe's hand, as it was the only familiar thing around.

"These are two different lives," Kufe said. "The blade is in one, and the hall of Records is in another."

"In the first life you saw," the avian explained, "Your sister was sacrificed. It was the first time you had ever seen her die, and it enraged you. You killed the priest who had killed her, and it was decreed that you would not see your partner for a while."

"How long was it?" I asked, still trembling.

"A few thousand years," Kufe replied. It seemed she also remembered this.

"Although you returned to her after the decreed time," the avian continued, "There remained an unpaid debt."

"Debt?" I asked. "What debt?"

"The priest you had killed," Kufe said. "He was yet to be appeased."

I remembered the words, '*The cycle would be completed, but I have not woven it to be this.*' I asked Kufe what they meant.

"You were hurt because I was taken away from you," Kufe said. "You knew you had no quarrel with the priest, yet you held him responsible for your pain. You struck back him... and took *him* away from his family too. Over time, a grievance was formed, which had to be repaid."

"Karma?" I scoffed.

"Yes, *Jefferson*," Kufe replied.

"An opportunity to appease the priest came soon enough," the avian continued. "You had decided to leave the Jewel, but did not want to wait until your form had aged. So you found another way."

I thought of the priest I had seen on the day I died. However, I didn't think he was responsible for my death – although granted, he was the last person who'd seen me alive.

"Not him," the avian said, and showed me an image from my recent memories: the license plate from the truck that had hit me.

"You both made an agreement," the avian said. "And he served his part. I hope you bear him no ill-will."

I'd never borne the driver any malice. Kufe smiled at me.

"So what's the third memory?" I asked.

"After you killed the priest," the avian said, "You remained away from your companion. When you had learned to stop pursuing vengeance, you came here and made this record. It was after this that you reunited with her."

I moved on to the third memory, and the light disappeared. I heard the words, "*I am the one who wanders through all...*" and suddenly the pale-blue ball of light appeared, hovering before me. I plucked it out of the air and handed it back to the avian.

"Thank you," Kufe smiled, and bowed slightly to the avian.

"It was good to see you again," he replied. "You both should visit more often."

"I will remind him," Kufe said.

"I must go now," he said. "There is always much to do." He spread his wings.

"Wait!" I stopped him. "What are these other pyramids for?"

He paused and, for a moment, I could swear he almost smiled at me. Of course, when you have a beak like that... it's hard to tell.

"They are *star gates*," the avian said, and with a powerful stroke of his wings, he rose into the air.

"Well, come on," Kufe urged, turning to me. "We're far from done."

"Okay," I said. "What now?"

"I'm on a vigorous campaign to reestablish your lost memories," she said. "There's much to be accomplished."

"And you plan to do this by mercilessly attacking everything I believe in," I said.

"Only the things you erroneously hold as truth," she corrected, and grabbed my wrist.

"Quantum leap! *Go!*" She exclaimed. Our surroundings changed.

"*Quantum Leap Go*?" I queried.

"We are in a different place now," Kufe said. "Here, you will find that things are more... *different*... than in other places."

"That makes no sense," I smiled. "Besides, what does this place have to do with 'Quantum Leaping'?"

"Oh, silence," she sighed. Grabbing my hand, she pulled me along with her.

"One of our friends is here," she said. "It's been a little while since we saw her."

"Who's she?" I asked.

"Our sister," Kufe replied. "A *star*."

10

This place was nothing like the last place we'd been. It was very exotic – I should say *psychedelic* – in appearance; colors swirled around in chaotic and harmonious patterns, rising from the various features of the already-bizarre landscape. The entire place seemed alive with energy – as if it were *all* living energy – and a very soft music filled the area.

A number of floating obelisks punctuated the endless landscape. As I passed each one, I noticed that they were covered in countless little squares. Occasionally, a new square would appear with a ticking sound.

"Do you remember the hall of Records?" Kufe asked.

I nodded; it was the second memory the avian had shown me.

"This place is like that," Kufe said, "But on a much larger scale."

"*Wow*," I gasped, looking around. "Who owns this one?"

Kufe made no reply. A short while later, we encountered a bright energy form. Unlike everyone else I'd met, I noticed that this form – this *being* – was clearly excited for no reason at all. It almost felt as though she was repeatedly proclaiming this to the Universe itself.

"Welcome!" the form greeted. "It's good to see you both!"

"It is good to see you too," Kufe smiled warmly.

"You are back from the Jewel!" the form exclaimed, addressing me. "How was that?"

"I hear it didn't go well," I sighed. "Critics say either, 'What are they doing down there?' or 'What did they do to you?'"

"He forgot much," Kufe explained. As the being laughed, I asked Kufe who she was.

"The star," she replied.

"Meaning, a celebrity?" I repeated. She searched me for the definition of the word, and shook her head.

"Remember when I told you that some stars live?" she asked.

"Yes," I replied. Kufe gestured broadly at the glowing being.

"But... *that's* not a star..." I said slowly.

"Hey, 'Quantum leap'?" Kufe said again. "I learned those words from *you*!"

"But you never explained what you meant!" I protested. "I don't know of *any* place where stars talk, or hang out in places this... this.... bizarre, and saying 'Quantum leap' doesn't explain anything!"

"We are in a different *dimension*, Jefferson," Kufe sighed. She turned back to grin at the star.

"Hello!" the star greeted again. Kufe briefly explained my memory issue to her.

"Unfortunate," she mused. "But not unusual."

"So, the Earth is screwed up," I shrugged. "What's new?"

"You know, I actually like the Jewel," the star told me.

I was surprised.

"Oh, I never went there," she said. "Its weavers can sometimes see me, though. I can't tell you how many wishes I process in a week."

"Wait," I said. "You grant wishes?"

"No," the star laughed, "But when you're like me, you can't avoid being wished on. Say, do you know what they call me?"

I was unsure of what star I was talking to.

"Uh... no..." I said, thinking on it. "Probably a Greek alphabet and a string of numbers. Like 'Alpha Prime four-seven-six.'"

"Whatever they *do* call me," she said, "I'm sure they find me -" It searched me for a word, "-*anomalous.*"

"Why?" I asked.

"I like to move around," she explained with a mischievous grin. "The others here don't move so much. I think *you* would move, too, if you were in my position."

"Other travelers?" I asked.

"Other stars," Kufe said. I faced the star.

"While I *don't* understand how you know a tiny planet that's light years away," I began, "I *should* punch you for making science more complicated than it needed to be. Do you realize how many theories will have to be formed to explain your behavior?"

"Some weavers should learn to let things be," the star laughed. "They think they are alone in the Universe, and they try to identify and label everything. They don't understand that not *everything* can be defined in a sentence."

She 'wagged a finger' at me.

"But I had nothing to do with…"

"*Nuclear fission*," Kufe said, cutting me off.

11

"Hey, why is Earth called the Jewel?" I asked. "Every time I hear that, it sounds like some sort of huge experiment."

"The Jewel was an experiment," Kufe said. "And in some ways, it still is."

"I should have known," I groaned.

"Look, if you observe any object and record its behavior," she said, "You have an experiment. Isn't this true?"

"But every experiment has a 'control,' against which the outcomes of the actual experiment are weighed," I argued. "Where's the 'control experiment' here?"

"*We* are," Kufe replied, spreading her arms. "Your Earth is a large experiment being observed by anyone who cares to. Whoever views it can only do so from their own perspective."

"If it wasn't organized," I said, "And if it isn't being monitored by a coordinated group, then it can't be called an experiment."

"If a tree... falls... in a forest..." Kufe began, peering at me. I made no reply.

"The Jewel has been through a lot," the star said. "It was once a fine world... but now, many only wish to destroy it."

"What do you mean?" I asked.

"The weavers of the Earth summon the things they fear," the star said. "They are afraid of being controlled – but they *believe* it will happen. As such, many beings who wish to control them are now approaching."

This was the stuff conspiracy theories were made of. I had laughed at such issues, while on Earth; now, I wasn't sure what to make of them. After all, I was being told this by a *star*.

"You still haven't explained why it is called the Jewel," I said. "What's so precious about it?"

"I can see the love you hold for that world," the star told me. "Did you look at it recently?"

I nodded, recalling my 'Post-Hell' experience.

"It's a beautiful place, isn't it?" the star asked.

"Well... yeah," I replied, "So, it's called the Jewel because it's pretty?"

"Only partially," Kufe said. "It is indeed a beautiful world, but its weavers are also important. They are powerful, and could become a very great race."

"This is true," the star assented, "But they don't seem to learn from their mistakes."

I remembered when Kufe told me that I was raised into a flawed system.

"It *is* flawed," the star said, picking my thoughts. "At this time, change will be very difficult."

"Why?" I asked.

"How many people were on the Jewel?" Kufe asked me.

"When I left," I said, "About six billion – and counting."

"Do you know what that means?" she asked.

"Nope," I replied. I didn't see any significance in that.

"You can tell a lot about a person by the way they think of others," the star giggled. She had caught my thoughts again.

"What's *that* supposed to mean?" I asked.

"In plain terms," she smiled, "You're stuck in your own world, and you can't see anything else."

"What are you two talking about?" I asked. "When did *I* become the bad guy?"

Kufe sighed, and turned to the star.

"Should we demonstrate?" she asked.

"Of course," the star giggled. To me, she added, "You may find the following images disturbing, partly because they require sporadic transformations, and partly because they are inspired by your memories."

I didn't have time to reply; Kufe had already assumed the visage of a King.

"Sire," the star bowed, "There are six billion people on a-"

"I must *conquer them all*!" Kufe roared, shaking her fist. Then she quickly changed into a priest's attire.

"Reverend," the star said, "There are six-"

"Why, we must *save* their souls!" Kufe sighed piously. "So many *souls*..."

She assumed another form; this time, a knight.

"*Armies!*" she cried, before the star could even speak again. They both burst out laughing, and Kufe reverted to her 'regular' form.

"Hey, Kufe," I said, "There are six billion people on Earth-"

"I know," she laughed. "You just told me."

"Then what was the point of..." I began.

"Six *billion* people, *Jefferson!*" she exclaimed, interrupting me. "Six billion threads and weavers on *one* world! It is difficult enough to stop one weaver, let alone six *billion*. The flaw in your system will remain until all the weavers stop to see what they have made."

"So what can be done?" I asked.

"Whatever *can* be done," Kufe replied.

"Like what, exactly?" I probed further.

"Tell them to stop and look," she shrugged. "But remember that warning a child against danger does not mean it will *avoid* danger."

"What does that have to do with..." I began.

"Give assistance freely," Kufe interrupted, "But don't consider yourself a failure when your assistance isn't accepted."

Now I understood what she meant. Also, she had a point. I felt hopeless. Kufe turned to the star.

"This been good," she said, "But we must leave now."

"Be sure to return," the star said. "Especially *you*. Visit when your memory comes back."

I nodded, and as Kufe squeezed my hand again, our surroundings gave way to the familiar landscape of the Pit Stop.

The Journey of Remembrance

12

I hadn't spoken to Kufe in a little while. She understood why.

"Jefferson," she said, "You already know the people and places you have seen."

"But I don't *know* that now!" I protested.

"'*He that knows, but does not know that he knows,*'" she said, peering at me, "'*He is confused. Teach him.*'"

"What's that from?" I asked. She stared at me quizzically.

"Shakespeare," she replied. "I took that from *you*."

I was unaware of that quote. Kufe laughed.

"You seem unable to remember many things," she smiled. "Words, places, people… star weavers!"

"But those things are impossible!" I protested.

"Only because you think of them as impossible," she replied.

"The things I know for sure are in conflict with the things I've seen, so far," I sighed. "In all my life, I…"

"In your *dream*," Kufe corrected, "And whatever you just learned there 'for sure' is as obsolete as what you learned there over four hundred years ago."

"Oh, *really*," I challenged. "Like what?"

"You were once ready to *prove* that the Jewel was flat," Kufe said.

"But the concept of a flat Earth is *outdated*."

"Indeed," she replied. "As is the concept of your Earth being the *only* populated planet in the Universe."

I remained silent. So far, there had been plenty of 'evidence' to support *everything* I had ever doubted. Why then, was it so hard to believe? I wasn't sure. Looking back on it, I understand now that I had still hoped to find a 'scientific' explanation for the things I'd seen. But, as the star had said, I needed to 'let things be.'

Kufe now approached and hugged me.

To be precise, it *started* like a hug – but soon, we completely merged forms. For what seemed like an eternity, I was a part of her, and I felt her as a part of me. In her memories, I saw myself – not as *Jeff*, but as many different people. I could neither recognize nor identify with a number of them, but that didn't matter.

At length, I felt Kufe squeeze my hand.

"We have one more place to go," she announced.

Still in a daze, I nodded.

"And on our next trip," she grinned, "*You* are doing all the talking."

As before, our surroundings melted away.

13

How can I describe where she took me next? It may be difficult for you to understand, but I'll try. It was an *empty* place; a void. There weren't any stars or planets, but I knew without doubt that it was part of our Universe.

Besides Kufe and I, the only other thing there looked like a gigantic, ethereal fountain. Instead of cascading water, little tendrils of light swirled around it in mesmerizing patterns. From a distance, the entire object looked enshrouded in a glowing mist.

If the pyramids had awed me, then I was completely *floored* by this 'fountain.' It seemed so profound that I immediately assumed it was some sort of god – which, of course, tripled my reluctance to approach it.

"No, *no*," Kufe whispered. "This is not a god."

I looked at it again and concluded that, if this 'fountain' thing appeared on Earth, about six billion people would immediately disagree with her.

"Go," Kufe whispered, nudging me forward.

"Where?" I asked.

"I told you," she said, "You're doing all the talking."

"*Why?*" I protested, and stole another glance at it. "It looks really busy."

"But it's not busy," Kufe replied.

"Look," I said hastily, "This thing... *lady*... guy..."

I paused, frustrated. In addition to being hard, assigning a gender to this thing also felt very wrong.

"*It* could probably kick my *asphalt* if I pissed it off..." I whispered. "You never know... it could be in the middle of something important...!"

"This will not happen," she replied again. "You are safe... *go!*"

"Well, what do I say?" I asked.

"A greeting might work," Kufe groaned. "*Now!*"

I conceded, and cautiously approached the 'fountain,' which I now saw was composed *entirely* of visible energy.

"Uh... *hi*," I waved, and promptly regretted it. Couldn't I have come up with something more appropriate?

"*Chet'zazu*," the fountain replied, suddenly glowing brighter. "*Kak'zau.*"

It changed form slightly, and I quickly retreated. I saw now that it was not a fountain, but another 'conscious' form of energy like everyone else I had encountered. I didn't understand what it had just said, and concluded it was upset by our intrusion. To my surprise, it began to laugh.

"Your hesitance is amusing," it said. "Those words had no meaning, and were only meant to confuse you. Come, now."

It 'beckoned' and I moved slightly closer. For a brief moment, it observed me.

"Who are you?" it asked.

"...Jeff," I replied, "*Jefferson* Hurley. I recently died... left Earth... the Jewel..."

The little tendrils of light put up a magnificent display; I could swear it had just chuckled.

"I see," it said. "And your companion?"

Kufe stepped forward.

"You!" it exclaimed happily, when it saw her. She smiled and proceeded to communicate privately with the being. When she was done, the being nodded, and focused on me.

"Welcome, *Jefferson*," it said, and its light reached to me. I suddenly felt like I'd been warmly hugged by a thousand people, and my fear melted away.

"Another old friend?" I asked Kufe.

"Well, it *is* old," she replied. "But no, not a friend in the way you think."

"Then who is it?" I asked.

"We can discuss it later," she sighed. "But you should speak to it."

I readied myself.

"Uh…" I turned to the being, "You know, since I *died*… left the Earth, I…"

"You are wondering what I am," the being offered.

"That's… yeah, that's what I was getting at," I said.

"Do you want the simple answer?" it asked.

"We can start there," I replied.

"I am a *Collective*," the being 'smiled.'

I gasped. *How*?

"The simple answer breeds more questions," it said. "Will you hear the longer answer?"

I nodded, too shocked to speak.

"Everything that exists is energy," it said, "Regardless of what form it chooses. My self, your self, your dream self, and your companion's – all are energy. Do you understand?"

I nodded.

"There was once a galaxy full of children," it said. "At first, they did not understand each other, but over time they learned how to play together. They finally united at heart, and later decided to do so in form.

"Now, they play as *one* child: one form containing the combined energy of many, *many* beings."

"A galaxy!" I gasped, "You… you're an entire *galaxy*?"

"Only the *children* of the galaxy," it corrected.

I couldn't compose any more coherent questions. Instead, I wondered how technologically advanced the civilizations of this galaxy must have been.

"Technology had its uses," the being said. "But it also had its disadvantages. In one way, it made many tasks easy. But some began to depend on it for survival – which is when it became a bad thing."

I thought about that.

"There were those," the being continued, "Who, like you, forgot much because of technology."

"How can that happen?" I asked.

"One weaves a dream for a certain amount of time," it replied, "Until that dream's purpose is accomplished. But if one first forgets the purpose of their dream, and then discovers a way to remain in the dream for an eternity…"

It said no more, and I understood perfectly.

"Did you…" I began. "Did the… *your* galaxy have people like that?"

"Yes," the being replied. "They all refused to take part in the transition and migrated well before the unification."

"Where did they go?" I asked.

"To many places," the being smiled. "I understand some even came to your world."

I waited for it to continue, but it said no more. I turned to Kufe again for assistance.

"You must understand," she whispered, "If you discovered these beings, then humanity could also find out and inadvertently seek them."

"I gather this would be a bad idea," I replied.

"A *very* bad idea," Kufe agreed. I turned back to the being, and mused that its existence required it to think constantly on a *Galactic* scale – far beyond my ability to comprehend, or so I thought. I felt very small, and couldn't help thinking again of the uproar it would cause if it went to Earth.

Speaking of Earth...

"Where *are* we?" I asked, looking around.

"Here," the being replied.

"*Here*?" I probed. "Where is 'here'?"

"An ancient and esoteric question," the being laughed, "One that ultimately proves useless when it's answered. We are on the other side of your Universe."

The Universe has another *side*? That caught me off guard. I wondered if this was where the Big Bang started from.

"Untrue," the being said. "We are *behind* your Universe."

Okay, I thought, *that* didn't make any sense.

"What do you mean?" I asked.

"This place defies your logic," the being replied. "Many such places exist – the center of the Universe, for instance – and by natural law, they are the *same* place. At this moment, I am the only one you see here because you both sought *me*. If you had come seeking any other being, you would find only them, as well. Do you understand?"

Completely lost, I said nothing; just stood there, in awe.

"Tell me of your world," the being requested.

I still made no reply.

"*Speak about your Earth*," Kufe whispered.

"Oh... *right*," I said, "Uh... not sure where to begin."

"Tell me what you know," the being said.

So I told him everything I knew about Earth. I pulled out every little bit of geography, history and philosophy I could think of, and even reached back to my conversations with my three friends. I finally concluded with the comments I'd heard about Earth since I left it.

"Ah," it said, "So you were one who wove on that world."

"Yeah…" I replied. "I mean, yes, I was there…"

"There are some who believe that world doesn't exist," the being chuckled. "And even others who do not even want to speak to that race. Your world is a strange place… Unusual things happen to the ones who go there."

Including me, I thought. Then I had an idea.

"I've heard we – *humans* – are in quite a predicament…" I stopped. Did I really think I could save the world by asking for help?

"I have assisted," the being reassured me. "At this time, many on that world do not desire assistance. All is well as it should be." It 'smiled' again, and I watched the little tendrils of light swirl around in glee.

"May we come again?" Kufe asked the being.

"As frequently as you desire," it replied warmly. I bowed to it – only because it felt appropriate – and it bowed back!

Kufe was smiling when she took my hand again.

14

We reappeared on the Pit Stop a moment later.
"So, how did that go?" Kufe asked me.
"Don't ever make me do that again," I replied.
"Do *what*?" she asked, genuinely confused.

I wasn't upset at her, but I *was* shaken by the experience. Think of it this way: how would you feel if you were to encounter a being that was infinitely older and wiser than you?

I sat on the rocky floor, and Kufe sat beside me.
"Where *was* that?" I asked.
"Nowhere," she replied. "It's not in this Universe."
"You know, I really don't get that," I sighed. "You can't say 'Nowhere' *and* 'It's not in this Universe.'"
"You can say that," she told me. "'Nowhere' is a collection of events, all localized in the same nonexistent place. Several different 'nowheres' cannot exist. Do you understand now?"

The more I questioned it, the less it made sense. However, there was no denying that I had seen this place – so it obviously existed. I accepted Kufe's statement for the moment.

"Fine," I said. "Where is 'nowhere'?"
"On the other side of *somewhere*," Kufe replied. "We are in 'somewhere,' right now. But like everything, it needs a polarity in order to exist: that would be 'nowhere.'"
"Isn't the *center* of the Universe a 'possible location'?" I asked.

"As possible as 'the edge of the Universe,'" she replied.

"But isn't that also..." I began.

"The Universe is mobile," Kufe interrupted. "Its center also varies with where you are. There is no *fixed* center or edge."

"*Mobile*?" I repeated. "The Universe *moves*?"

"Constantly," she said. "Expanding, contracting, rotating; if it's not moving, then something is moving within it."

The concept was completely alien to me.

"The Universe is not solid," Kufe continued. "It is comprised of multiple dimensions, with each one unique in its characteristics. This is why they move at different speeds."

That sounded like the planet Jupiter's rotation, I thought. Its bands moved at different speeds, didn't they?

"It is much the same, yes," Kufe replied. "But this is not to suggest that the Universe has a *shape*. Remember also that these dimensions exist *within* each other, not above and below."

I decided not to question her. I decided not to question *anything* anymore. I realized – for the last time – that Jefferson Hurley was dead.

There was a flash of light, and I saw myself as a child again. Ah, the carefree days of innocence... I longed for them. I could only long for a moment, because the images were quickly replaced by my adolescent years. I watched, spellbound, as my entire life played out before me. I realized just how tiny Jefferson Hurley appeared in the face of the Universe *I* had come to discover. I saw that my doubt had bordered on the fanatic 'blind faith' I had so passionately despised in my lifetime.

As abruptly as it appeared, the light vanished. I was left on the floor, staring up at the stars, and I felt very tired.

"I need to rest," I told Kufe. She cradled my head in her lap, and I fell asleep.

I eventually awoke to find myself in Kufe's arms. I was touched that she was still there... then I noticed we weren't at the Pit Stop anymore. Above me stretched the bluest skies I had ever seen, perfectly complementing the familiar, lush green grass below me.

"Did you rest well?" Kufe asked. I nodded, speechless, and sat upright to view my surroundings. This was a beautiful place – in a way that I could immediately appreciate. The grass grew low around me, and all the way to the shore of a placid lake. On the other side of this was a picturesque blue mountain range. Behind me, the grass stretched to the horizon.

"Man," I said, "It would *really* suck if it started raining."

It was all I could think of. Kufe laughed, and rose to her feet.

"Let's play," she said, pulling me up. "It's been a long time, and you need the exercise."

I couldn't resist the idea; the weather was perfect, and I didn't have to work anymore. What else was there to do? After explaining and initiating a game of 'tag,' we were soon running around like children. We laughed as loudly as we could for no reason at all, and I romped around with an energy unlike anything I had ever known.

I think it was actually the first time I had ever felt *good*.

15

Kufe and I raced to the lake. I beat her to it and dove in. She stopped at the edge.

"Come on in!" I invited. "The water's perfect!"

She cautiously dipped a toe into the water and smiled. Then she lifted her toe out of the water and placed it gingerly on the surface again. Carefully, she moved her weight onto the toe, until she stood – on tiptoe – on the lake. She took several steps forward.

"You know," I sighed, looking up at her, "Several million people on Earth are *really* mad at you right now."

She caught the joke and smiled. As I watched, she dropped through the warm surface of the water. Soon, we were floating next to each other.

"Why can't I remember anything?" I asked.

"You have," Kufe sighed. "But not much."

"But I tried," I protested, "And I haven't hit on *anything*."

"You searched the wrong place," she told me. "You're still searching *Jefferson*. You cannot see outside him because you are not looking outside him."

"What do you mean?" I asked.

"Think back to the Library," she said. "What do you see?"

I knew she wasn't asking about *what* the avian had shown me. She wanted to know how I'd felt about what I'd seen. I thought about it.

"*Jefferson's* experiences," I replied thoughtfully.

"You viewed them as Jefferson's dreams, and not your memories," Kufe said. "But these things are *real*."

"How can I get *past* Jefferson?" I asked. She smiled and floated closer to me.

"You have to *let go* of him," she said. "Your judgment forced you to review your life badly. You have to view it again – but honestly, this time."

"Will you help?" I asked.

"Certainly," she replied.

"Great," I breathed. "How do I do this?"

"When you left the dream," Kufe said, "You did not know you were dreaming. Now you do: begin again from where you told me. This time, I will view your dream with you"

I thought back to the night of the accident. The memories returned in sequence, and I was able to view them with clarity now. It felt now as though it were a bad dream.

"I'm going to have a *lot* of questions," I warned Kufe.

"I know," she smiled, and took my hand again.

Much later, we watched as I 'discovered' my ability at the hospital.

"You know," I told Kufe. "I was really hoping I would be able to keep that when I recovered."

"Well, you have it now," she replied. "I find it surprising that you don't have the ability on the Jewel. Many weavers there are self-conscious. They wrap their identity very tightly around themselves, and they project it so loudly that one cannot help but notice."

"Are you saying humans are self-centered?" I asked.

"Sometimes," she replied. I remembered what Jack told me: Even the Collective had known my name.

"Yeah," I sighed. "I guess you're right."

"Your weavers feel a need to constantly identify themselves, and everything around them," Kufe said. "They will label *anything* they come across. Fortunately, you have learned."

"I *learned* something?" I repeated, surprised. Kufe indicated everything around us, and I realized that I hadn't yet asked her what this place was called. I surmised that it probably didn't have a name anyway.

"Now, do you understand?" Kufe asked. I nodded.

"Good," she smiled, "We're getting somewhere."

We kept watching my memories. Soon, we arrived on the day of my death.

"You don't have to view what follows," she told me. "If you choose, you can leave it for another time."

"I'm sure I'll be fine," I said. "Besides, I have to do this sometime." Kufe patted my hand, and we returned to the vision before us. When we got to the Tremendous Being, I started laughing.

"That guy is *huge*," I said. The scene paused, and we observed the Tremendous Being and the two unknown witnesses.

"I wonder what caused you to create him," Kufe mused.

"Well, when you learn about 'God' in the way I did," I said, "You can't help thinking that he's that large. Songs like *'He's got the whole world in his hand'* didn't help, either."

Kufe observed the scene.

"It's funny," I continued. "By the time you're a teenager, you think about God in three ways: You love him, hate him, or don't believe in him."

"*Him*," Kufe repeated. "And what do you think of 'him' now?"

I didn't reply immediately. It wasn't because I was unwilling to consider the question. Everything regarding Jefferson's life still felt like a dream, but besides that, I couldn't remember anything else.

"I'm... not sure," I apologized.

"You don't remember," Kufe smiled. "But I know you're close."

"Well, *that's* a relief," I said. We turned to the frozen scene.

"Who were those guys?" I indicated the blurry witnesses. Kufe peered at them.

"They are *you*," she said.

"That's not possible," I protested. "For starters, I didn't like them."

"And you 'like' yourself?" she asked.

"More than them!" I replied.

"But you punished yourself," she pointed out. "Your witnesses were manifestations of two extremes you had come to hate. When the large one called for witnesses, what did you think?"

I thought back to the moment.

"I... knew it was going to be an unfair judgment," I replied slowly.

"So you sent forward what you thought he was expecting," Kufe said. "You gave him the 'good' and the 'bad' you thought he would see."

"You're saying I *made* those guys?" I gasped.

"Including the large one," she nodded. "You made *everything* you saw before you left the inferno."

"But why did I judge myself that harshly?" I asked. "If I created my own judge, wouldn't I be more forgiving towards myself?"

"That depends on how well you know yourself," she said, patting my hand again. "Jefferson had several deep misgivings that he never confronted."

I thought about this.

"I'll remember not to do it again," I said.

"Lesson learned," Kufe cheered.

Much later, we walked away from the lake. The farther we got, the higher the grass grew, until it covered our ankles. Shortly, we arrived at a steep precipice. At its bottom lay more grass, which stretched as far as the eye could see. I smelled the ocean far away, and a gentle breeze caressed us both. It felt *perfect*.

"It's much easier to create, out here," I heard Kufe say. "I'm glad you like it."

I understood what she meant, and I was even more spellbound. She had *created* this place.

"For you," she said. "Because you needed it."

"How?" I asked.

"It's a bridge from your former world," she explained. "It feels familiar, because it looks like the Jewel. You can rest in it, because you know you are safe; you can also return to it when you want to."

I stared out to the horizon, and took a deep breath of the clean air.

"How can you care so much for someone who doesn't remember you?"

"How can you not?" Kufe replied, and took my hand again.

16

We returned to sit by the lake, and concluded my review. Kufe cringed when the images of Hell appeared. I too was aghast at what I saw. I hadn't realized how bad it was.

"This place was also built from your expectations," she said, and made a face. "How can one even *create* this?"

"I guess I was worse off than I thought," I said to her. She was watching the scene intently – a difficult task, since she was repulsed by what she saw.

"It seems that only this place grew worse, over time," she told me, "While your witnesses were forgotten somewhere in your childhood."

She was right. As a child, my vision of Hell had been much more tame than the sight before us. This also explained the ridiculous charges leveled against me by the first witness.

"It would help," Kufe said, "if you were as honest with yourself as with the ones around you. That way, you don't carry such horrors..." Her words trailed off, but I understood what she meant.

Kufe stopped viewing the images. "Is there anything else you need to see?"

"Well, two things happened," I told her, and showed the moment when I 'appealed' my case in Hell.

"This was the first big thing that happened," I said. She watched, and then probed me for an explanation of the Ten Commandments.

"Jack would *love* this," she smiled.

"You still haven't told me who he is," I said. She waved it off.

"What was the second thing?"

"This," I said, and showed her the moment of my 'awakening.' She watched in relief as the vision of Hell was ripped apart, and gasped when she saw the Earth.

"That must have been a welcome sight," she said.

"It was better than the previous one," I replied. "You know, I suddenly realize that seeing the Earth was a sort of joke; even after days when I *hated* Earth, I saw it as 'Heaven' in comparison to another place."

"Then, your 'Heaven' and your 'Hell' were real," she replied. "They were just not what you thought they would be."

"So, if I chose neither," I said, "Then where have I gone?"

"Home," Kufe said simply.

"Where's that?" I asked.

"*Here*," she replied, and hugged me. We merged again, and when we came apart, she laughed.

"This is the first time I have seen a review that stretched past the moment of death," she said. "You were always an unusual one."

"What can I say?" I shrugged. "I try."

"And now," she breathed, "For the most important question you have asked, since you came out."

"What was that?" I asked.

"'Who is Jack?'" she replied.

"About time," I said. "What's with the mystery?"

"In order to find out who he is," Kufe said, "We have to get him here."

"Okay," I said.

"It is only fair," she smiled. "We can't discuss him in his absence. He can best tell us about himself."

She turned to stand by me.

"Hey, Jack!" she called.

Jack appeared before us, on the grass. He was wearing a towel and holding a razor.

"*Whoa! hey!*" he exclaimed. "Bad timing."

Jack

Jack

7

"Hello Jack," Kufe smiled.

"It is always good to see you," he chuckled. "Hey, kid," he turned to me. The towel vanished, replaced by an impressive ankle-length robe.

"Hey, Jack," I said. "We were just talking about you." I eyed the robe warily.

"Whatever you heard is not true," Jack grinned, and patted me on the shoulder.

"Well, that's the problem," I said. "I haven't heard anything."

"Then you weren't ready," he shrugged.

"I'm ready now," I replied.

"I know," he smiled. "That's why I came." He patted my shoulder again.

"Well," I queried, "Who *are* you?"

"'Don't rightly know,'" he chuckled.

"Oh for *God's* sake!" I sighed.

"I can tell you a lot about myself," he laughed, "But that won't tell you *who* I am. Do you know who you are?"

"What the… of *course* I know *who* I am!" I shot back.

"Oh, okay," he nodded, and walked a short distance away. Kufe started laughing.

"Am I missing something?" I asked. Kufe turned to me.

"I should explain…" she began.

"Why are you guys being all weird about this?" I asked her. "Is it such a big deal?"

"Well," Kufe said, "Jack is one of the many representations of *absolute* knowledge."

I waited for her to continue, but she didn't.

"And?" I asked.

"Look at him," she said. I turned to look at Jack; He was now singing to a little bird. At the end of his performance, he bowed, and the bird flew off.

"Yeah," I said, "I get that he's sort of… weird."

"He knows *everything* that exists," Kufe said. "He knows everything about you and I, and everyone else you have ever met."

"Wait," I gasped, "You mean he's…"

Smiling, Jack strode back towards us. As he approached, I now sensed in him the same wisdom that I had felt with the Collective.

"Jefferson," Jack said, "I am your *Cousin*."

I blinked.

"Cousin?"

"I made a pop-culture reference," he grinned. "And stop acting so surprised. If *you* can exist, I think I can, too."

I stared at him.

"There was a time," he said, "When nothing was known – because nothing existed. The question, 'Who am I?' rang through the stillness, and in that moment, *everything* was born."

A dark sphere appeared. I soon realized it was a miniature simulation of space.

"You should tell that to the proponents of the Big Bang theory," I said, watching the display.

"I tried," Jack sighed. "They wouldn't even let me in the door." The hologram disappeared, and he put an arm around my shoulder.

"The only real difference between you and me," he confided, "is that you work to fill a Universal Library. I *am* that Library."

2

I stared at Jack, still trying to assemble what he'd just said.

"So, if you're *God*..." I began.

"Who said I was?" he replied. "I'm not *God* any more than Krishna is."

"*Krishna?!*" I repeated. Another being appeared beside us, waved hello, and promptly vanished.

"He's really busy," Jack apologized. "Look kid, I'm just a representation of all the knowledge that exists. Remember when I told you that I know my way around?"

"Well, I *do*," I said, "But *still*..."

Jack morphed into Jefferson Hurley. I hadn't seen 'myself' since the hospital, and I felt slightly uncomfortable again.

"I can do *this*," Jack explained, "Because all the information that exists about this character-" he indicated his new visage, "-exists in *me*." His attire switched back to the impressive robe.

"In conclusion, I am not *God*," he said. "I am not *God*. I am what God knows. I'm still a sub-characteristic, like you."

"So..." I said slowly, "You just *know* everything..."

"But I am *not* everything," he agreed.

"Well!" I exclaimed. "Didn't you just tell me *who* you are?"

"No," he replied. "Excuse me."

He created a large leather chair and sat in it. Kufe sat on the grass by his feet, and I sat beside her.

"Okay," I said, "I have a *lot* of questions. Since you're the guy with answers, I'm assuming you can answer all of them?"

"Only the ones you need," he replied.

Fair enough, I thought, and gathered my queries.

"Let's start with this. I'm still wondering about that judgment thing. Kufe told me that I had created those guys… every part of it – but how could I create something that wasn't in my control?"

"But it *was* in your control," Jack replied. "You destroyed what you created, didn't you?"

"I did," I agreed. "But why didn't I recognize it from the start?"

"Because you can play elaborate practical jokes on your mind," he said.

"But why would anyone do that?".

"The need arises," Jack explained. "You're taught to fear a thing, because it can kill you. You later believe that it exists for the sole purpose of destroying you. At that point, your mind hides it from you in order to protect you.

"Now, if you were able to create that creature, what's the first thing it would do?"

He waited for an answer.

"It kills you?" I asked.

"It *tries* to kill you," he corrected. "Sure, it can hurt you… but it can't kill you, because you made it. It can't function without your existence. It's *your* fear. You can remove it, but you don't remember that because…"

"…You fear it," I completed. This made plenty of sense. Excited now, I dug up more questions.

"What happens when you undo your creation?" I said, after a moment's pause. "Where do they go?"

"The same place they came from," Jack replied. "The realm of possibility."

"But isn't that what *you* are?" I asked.

"You're catching on," he smiled. "Interestingly, that makes me the most beautiful and the most terrifying thing in existence."

That got me thinking. To my recollection, 'God' had been defined in similar terms. If Jack embodied every possibility, and yet *wasn't* God…

"What's the difference between you and the… commonly-accepted definition of 'God'?" I asked.

"Aha!" he exclaimed, "You want *science!*"

I was confused. Kufe laughed.

"The actual difference between myself and what you call 'God' is great," said Jack. "The difference between myself and your definitions… is not so great."

"Go on," I urged.

"I told you about the moment when everything was born, didn't I?" He created the sphere once more.

"Watch closely. We will soon have the primary event…"

He paused, for effect.

"And *whoosh*!"

I watched an explosion of light in the center of the sphere. The light spread through the sphere, eventually forming little dots at its extremities. Jack pointed at one of the dots.

"'Jeff H.' is a sub-characteristic of one of those," he said; "A true son of light, as with everyone who left the primary event. Now, for the secondary event: *Creation!*"

The little dots of light moved around fitfully, much unlike the orderly, linear emigration pattern that I expected.

"As the little sparks of consciousness explore their new playground," Jack announced, "Civilizations are born."

The activity within the hologram thinned, and I saw the tiny galaxies again. Intermittently, streaks of light appeared between the 'stars.' I couldn't tell if these were either natural or artificial objects.

"And now," Jack said, "Regarding the difference between your 'God' and I. There's one part we haven't seen."

A three-dimensional grid appeared around the sphere, like a tennis ball hovering in a wireframe cylinder.

"Hypothetically speaking," Jack explained, "This grid is our knowledge base. Look at it closely."

I did, and saw tiny electrical impulses flashing along it.

"Those flashes represent information," he said. "By which I mean everything it knows, and everything *you* need to know about *it*. Remember; this grid is still a *property* of this Universe."

He pointed to an area where the sphere touched the grid. There, a transparent bubble extracted itself from the point of contact.

"And thus," he said solemnly, "I was born."

"Hey," I said, "How come *you* get to be a transparent bubble?"

"Because the bubble can do *this*," Jack replied. The bubble morphed into a comet, and instantly shot off into the miniature Universe.

"Infinite possibilities, my friend," he sighed. "'Jack' is just one thing this bubble can do. Now, do you understand?"

I nodded slowly.

"So," I said, "I am a by-product of light…"

"You *are* the light," Jack corrected.

"And you are a transparent bubble," I continued.

"Precisely," he replied. "A bubble that represents a grid, which is a property of a larger object."

"So, where is *God*, exactly?" I asked.

Jack smiled and pointed at the hologram.

"The energy that caused the explosion was released into the 'universe.' It is embedded in everything in the form of energy molecules, like cells in living organisms. This energy is conscious and *everywhere*. That's where God is."

Jack

3

I stared at the hologram, and I suddenly understood what Jack was saying. I'd never come across a description of God like that. It seemed rather attractive, but it brought up other concerns.

"If there's a *conscious* 'God'…" I began.

"I know what you're thinking," Jack said. "But no; this isn't like your Judge."

"Then how is it?" I probed.

"Imagine that this," he pointed at the hologram, "is a *brain*." The sphere took on the shape of a brain, and the grid remained as a two-dimensional aspect of its surface.

"Everything that happens inside this brain," he continued, "Can be registered as a little flash of electricity. For instance…"

Corresponding flashes occurred on the brain.

"*We* are the flashes," Jack said. "'God' is the brain."

He waited to see if I understood.

"Nope," I told him. "I still don't get it."

"Think of it this way," he said, "We are a functioning aspect of the larger totality. One of the underlying purposes of our existence is 'interactions with the whole.' But first, we want to find out *what* the whole is. As such, we all explore to discover what the Universe is. We are a part of each other, and we are all to go through this discovery together. That is the 'unification' you heard about."

I remembered the Collective.

"But clearly, there are other advanced cultures out there," I argued. "Couldn't they all have discovered what the Universe is, at this point?"

"You're thinking of space," Jack said. "Heads up!"

The hologram disappeared, along with our cozy surroundings. We were left hovering in space.

"This is *three* dimensional *space*," he said, "Sometimes called 'The Observable Universe.' It isn't *The* Universe, though."

"Where do other dimensions come in?" I asked.

"When you move," he replied. The lights around us blurred, and then completely disappeared.

"Welcome," Jack said, "To another part of your Universe."

I was awestruck. This place looked *nothing* like the 'universe' I was familiar with.

The furthest reaches of this 'space' faded into a vibrant blue, and a bright light with no apparent source illuminated our location within it.

Please forgive the sketchy description. If I could describe this place in more detail, I would. Sadly, the appropriate words don't exist on Earth.

"Things are different here," Jack told me. "The beings here are more logically-acute than humans because, in developing, their minds come to accommodate the complexity of their versatile natural surroundings."

"Is that a nice way of saying that humans are dumb?" I queried.

"Compared to the Weavers here?" Jack replied, "*Yes.*"

We moved to a beautiful galaxy, peppered with colors I didn't think I could ever find in space. Within it, we went to a radiant, pale blue star system. I hadn't even *known* stars came in that shade of blue.

"Do you recognize this?" Jack asked me.

"Nope," I replied, "But it looks awesome."

"Look carefully," he suggested.

I now realized that this system shared the same number and distribution of major planets as Earth's solar system. There was even a gigantic Jovian where Jupiter was supposed to be! Nonetheless, this was the only similarity I could find here.

"Exactly," Jack said, responding to my thoughts. I did a double take. Was this *really* Earth's Solar system in another dimension of the Universe? Was that even possible? I turned to Jack, and he shrugged, as if to say, "*Anything* is possible."

"The three dimensional existence you're familiar with is an aspect of this dimension," he said. "As you can see, familiar objects look and act very differently here."

"Is the Earth... populated?" I asked in surprise.

"Well of *course* the Earth is populated," Jack scoffed. "Next, you'll be asking me if it's flat..."

"No! Wait... I..." I spluttered. "I mean *this* planet!"

"Ah!" Jack exclaimed, "Then why didn't you say so?"

"I *did*!" I protested.

"But you called it *Earth*," he pointed out.

"*Whatever* it's called," I sighed. "Is there anything on it?"

"Yes there is," he smiled.

We reappeared on the grassy plain, in our familiar Universe – I should say 'dimension.' The hologram awaited us.

"I have one more question," I eventually said. "All this time, you've used a sphere as a 'visual aid'... but I heard the Universe doesn't actually *have* a shape, and it... and it moves... what does the *real* Universe look like?"

"You *really* don't want to know," Jack winked.

"Oh, come on," I sighed. "I'm not a kid."

"Alright," he laughed. "...But you asked for it."

He pointed at the sphere, and it began to undulate. A moment later, it vanished.

"Oh, it's still there," Jack said. His chair reappeared, and he sat in it. "This isn't the *actual* form of our Universe, but it gives you a pretty good impression of what it looks like."

"Can *you* see it?" I asked Kufe. She shook her head.

"You're saying I'm the *only* one here who sees it?" Jack gasped. "Goodness... you're both looking at it from the *wrong* angle!"

"Oh!" Kufe exclaimed, and smiled. "I see it now."

I looked where the hologram had been, but I still couldn't see anything.

"Do you want to see it?" she asked me.

"I'm *allowed* to see it?" I asked.

"Of course," Jack replied. "But it's not going to mean much."

"I'll be the judge of that," I replied, and turned to Kufe. "What do I do?"

She took my hand.

"Keep your eye on that spot," she said, pointing where the hologram had been. I nodded again, and our surroundings melted.

When we reappeared by Jack, moments later, I was screaming.

Jack

    With some assistance, I calmed down. However, I was unwilling to think about what I had just seen. I had to remind myself that I *did*, in fact, ask for it.

    "Next time," Jack chuckled, "Don't ask a question if you're not ready for the answer."

    "I'll remember that," I promised.

    "I'm sure you will," he grinned. "So, you're probably wondering what that was."

    I hastily thought of anything *but* the shape.

    "I'll explain it simply for you," he said. "Some objects can only exist in higher dimensions. If they were to interact with a lower dimension, they would be invisible. What you saw exists across several dimensions – which is why you had to move in order to see it."

    I nodded again. To my surprise, he created a pipe and stuck it in his mouth.

    "You know," I said, "Smoking causes cancer."

    "Doesn't it?" he smiled. "It's funny you mention that, because I was just thinking about how *humans* act like a cancer."

    "How?" I asked.

    "They are isolated," Jack said. "They think they are alone, and they act like it. And no matter *what* you do, you can't wipe them out because they keep coming back. I suppose they act more like a *virus* than anything…"

"Wait, are you saying that some beings have tried to wipe humans out before?" I asked in shock.

"Mm... *Maybe*," he drew out.

"When was this?!" I exclaimed. "*Aliens* seriously tried to wipe out the Earth?"

"That word, *aliens*," Jack grimaced, "There's something about it that I don't like."

"Oh, you *know* what I mean!" I shot back.

"Right, right," Jack said, and chewed on his pipe thoughtfully. "You have to understand that the human race is a very powerful one. In the past, a race of humans made a lot of friends, as well as enemies."

"Yeah, I've *heard* that before," I said, "But I still don't get it."

"The culture of the 'human race' has existed for a long time," Jack said, "Even older than its current civilization remembers."

"Still, what makes them so unique?" I asked. I expected to hear something outrageous, for instance, the Moon was really a *weapon*... or that Earth was the last frontier in a battle against an ancient god, who would soon awake...

Jack laughed at my train of thought.

"Ironically, it's their ability to *love*," he said. "The one thing they're having trouble doing as a group."

That's not outrageous, I thought; that's *ridiculous*.

"I'm serious," he insisted. "From the first civilizations they raised, they were an astounding group; they were *passionate*. This was comparatively rare, because most of the other beings had transcended passion..."

"You mean, they became unemotional?" I asked.

"In a manner of speaking," Jack agreed, "But you should remember that an unemotional person isn't always cold and amoral. A lack of emotion allows for better empathy and less attachment."

"Better empathy?" I repeated. "Would that person even *care* about anything?"

"Of course they would," Jack replied. "Without an emotional burden, one can afford to be very objective."

I saw what he meant.

"But that's the thing," he continued. "Humans are persistent. They want to bring their emotion with them. They get passionate about everything. Then their civilizations fall, and they survive... and do it all over again."

I turned to Kufe and asked, "Is that the flaw?"

"How can you stop them?" she replied softly. I couldn't see

their point. What was so wrong with emotion?

"It's not just about *having* emotion," Jack corrected. "Human passion can make for interesting times – don't get me wrong – but it can also get in the way."

"Give me an example," I said.

"Alright," Jack said. "Name *one* big event in your Earth's common history."

I thought for a moment.

"Lunar landing…" I replied.

"*Wrong*," Jack said emphatically.

"Hey man," I warned, "Don't knock the landings. 'One giant leap for mankind…'"

"The lunar landing was not a combined effort from the entire planet," Jack replied.

"But it was *significant* for the planet," I argued.

"Oh, you're right!" Jack exclaimed, and sighed. "Silly me… how could I forget? Why, the flag of *Earth* was put up there for all to see…"

He shook his head sadly.

"To think that I'm supposed to know these things," he sighed. "I think I'm getting old."

Jack

5

I made no comment.

"Come on," Jack nudged, "You haven't named anything yet."

"Fine," I sighed. "World War Two."

"Exactly," Jack smiled. "It *has* to be a war. So far, humans have only shared events that involve violence."

"Gloat all you want," I groaned. "What about the Olympics? That's not usually a violent…"

"Munich, 1972," Jack interrupted. I decided not to argue.

"Back to the war. What part did emotion play?"

"One man was passionate about bringing his country – and race – to glory," Jack shrugged. "He wasn't *evil*. Sure, his acts made him a little detestable… but still, he's not evil. *Anyone* could be him, if they had enough cause."

"But wouldn't he have been worse if he *didn't* have emotion?" I asked. "Wouldn't that make him more ruthless? Don't the nature of his crimes denote a cold nature?"

"No," Jack said, "If he'd been dispassionate about his causes, you would never have heard of him."

"Why is that?" I asked.

"Because he wouldn't rise to power," Jack replied. "He wouldn't think there was anything great about ruling the world."

This made sense.

"So why didn't… why doesn't… *God* step in?" I asked. "I mean, you said he… *it*… conscious energy…"

"And I also said, 'Humans, *cancer.*'" Jack smiled. "What you call 'God' is as objective as the Universe it created. Everything that exists is capable of functioning independently, or as part of a whole. Humans, right now, are functioning independently. They have to start functioning as part of a whole." He morphed on a tie-dye shirt.

"Then why don't *you* go there?" I asked. "People would listen to you, wouldn't they?"

"Nope," he replied. "They called me a... *hippie*. Not that I care; I rather like this shirt."

"Jack wouldn't be the first to be ignored," Kufe now said, "Many others have gone to that world, yet no one listened."

"People listened to Jesus, didn't they?" I protested. After a moment's pause, I added, "He was *real*, right?"

Jack blew out a cloud of smoke, although he never lit the pipe.

"People took his story and beat themselves to a bloody pulp with it. They're *still* doing it."

"So, what's the real story?" I asked. Jack created and tossed me a ball.

"What's this?" I asked.

"A ball," Jack shrugged. "Do you want to hear the story or not?"

"Well... yeah!" I exclaimed.

"Then keep the ball moving," Jack replied. I obliged, and tossed the ball back to him.

"Once upon a time..." he began.

I sat still, when Jack completed his tale. I had since stopped returning the ball.

"Quite profound, wasn't it?" Jack asked, with the air of a pious preacher. "Compare *that* to what you know."

"The differences are astounding!" I gasped.

"That's why no one approaches Earth with bells and whistles anymore," he sighed. "Back in time, humans would worship you for a few years. These days, they want to dissect everything that moves."

"Or worse," Kufe shuddered, "They make *weapons* out of you."

Jack

6

The gravity of the situation finally hit me.

There were six billion people potentially as confused as I had been. These people didn't know that everything they learned was only partially true; they were staring at the sun for guidance, unaware they should use the sun's light to guide themselves. This was the analogy used to explain my predicament when I first left Hell, and I actually understood it for the first time.

"You're catching on," Jack winked.

I revisited the moment after I left Hell, when I appeared above the Earth. I saw the watchers again, This time, I watched the ones compiling reports.

"So the Earth really *is* an experiment," I said.

"Not in the way you think," Jack replied. "Do you remember the memories you were shown?"

I did.

"Review them in order," Jack said. "Tell me about them."

I reviewed the first and the second, and what I'd been told about them. The third didn't fit anywhere yet.

"Two were connected," I replied. "I killed someone in the first memory, and I wasn't allowed to see Kufe until the second."

"Do you *remember* why you couldn't see her?" he probed. I could see he was pushing me to actually remember the events as they occurred. With new resolve, I forced myself past any lingering traces of Jefferson Hurley and focused on the first memory. I caught glimpses of Earth in a very distant past – and believe me, things looked really different. I knew this was the time when I killed the priest. I watched the events progress. Years after the deed was committed, I 'died.' I subsequently stood before a group of slightly upset beings. It was unclear who they were, but what I saw was nothing like the 'Tremendous Being' encounter. It was quite obvious that I *hadn't* invented this tribunal. I now remembered how the avian had kept saying 'It was decreed'... Who were these beings to decree anything?

"Who *are* these guys?" I asked, still watching the scene.

"The first Council of Elders," Jack replied. "The scouts you saw were compiling reports for them."

"Was there more than one?" I asked.

"The first Council evolved, and subsequently re-assimilated into the system," Jack replied. "However, it continues its duties in varying forms – and I mean that literally."

I remembered Kufe saying, "*You won't believe how many people were sent into the dream by others...*"

It suddenly made sense – or at least, I thought it did. Jack had said that the ultimate purpose of our existence was to interact with others, right? So, maybe these 'Elders' occasionally generated beings to go to Earth, in order to 'test' the people that were already there. That would be why they created scouts to monitor the goings-on. Could this possibly account for the numerous 'gods' in Earth's old religions?

"No," Jack sighed. "However, I must commend you on discovering how Conspiracy Theories are made."

I'd again forgotten that Jack was fully synchronized with my thoughts.

"Think of *Doctors*," he offered.

"*Doctors*," I repeated. "Very nice suits. What about them?"

"They all share the same duties," he said, "But their tasks are overseen by a Board of Peers. Did you know this?"

"Vaguely," I replied, "But go on."

"Of course, in order to be an overseeing peer," he continued, "You have to stand out. Do you see what I mean?"

"You're saying these were *accomplished* spirits?" I asked.

"Elites, specially issued directly from the Source." Jack replied. "In those first days, a tangible guiding presence was needed to oversee what was done, and determine what was acceptable and unacceptable. Thus, the Council was formed – not as a panel of judges, but as a representative group that would generate the rules of the game. When things got better, they merged with the all again, occasionally producing avatars to roam the madness."

"In other words" I said. "You are an avatar of the Council?"

"You could say that," Jack replied. "But remember; we aren't independent gods, and we never refer to ourselves as such."

I nodded.

"So who made the Earth an experiment?"

"You're still thinking subjectively," Jack sighed. "What you *want* to hear is that your Earth is at the mercy of something or other. Hard fact: it *isn't*."

"Whoever observes the Jewel can only do so from their perspective," Kufe said. "I told you that."

"She's right," Jack said. "As I said, the current civilization acts like a disease. Some beings are monitoring it to see what it turns into."

"To determine if preventive measures need to be taken?" I asked.

"Not necessarily," Jack laughed, "Although that's exactly what would happen if *some* people were in charge of things…"

I personally couldn't see any solution besides a preemptive strike against Earth. Don't get me wrong; I wasn't advocating this in any way. My sister still *lives* there, as do my friends.

Try to see it from my standpoint – or rather, Jack's (and the rest of the Universe's) perspective. As part of a large community, you wouldn't want to *destroy* one person because they were causing some trouble. You would know that harming that person would equate to harming your own community; as such, you would find an alternate method of dealing with the issue. As I understood it, this was what was being carried out with Earth.

New images appeared before me – this time, involuntarily. I looked at them, puzzled. They appeared to be more memories from the time I killed the priest.

"What's going on?" I asked. The images continued.

"Well," Jack replied, "It looks like your memory is coming back."

Jack

A thick cloud cover hid the sky. I knew this was long ago; probably farther back than you'd be willing to believe. Even the *plants* looked different. This was probably because the Earth's atmosphere – or its entire ecosystem – was different from the last one I'd seen.

The cozy surroundings of Kufe's gift had melted away, and I now stood on the landscape of an ancient, forgotten Earth. I wasn't frightened by this; I was *excited* by it. There was a feeling of power again, like I'd felt before I destroyed my Hell. In fact, I was so elated that I spread my 'arms' and tore through the evening sky.

My companions followed. Kufe had taken the form of an eagle, and soared beside me. Jack was flying too; however, he was doing this in his large leather chair, now equipped with a plane's control wheel. He was doing his best to keep up with the high wind.

"What?" he asked, when he noted that I'd been staring at him. "This is nothing! Back in the war, I used to fly *jets!*"

I grinned. Of course, Jack had never flown a fighter jet. But there was no doubt that he knew how: he knew *everything*.

Much later, we sat on a cliff, overlooking a savanna.

"Is *this* an actual memory?" I asked Kufe.

"In a way," she replied. "You have reconstructed the entire planet as you remembered it."

"I did *what*?" I gasped.

"This is just a tiny moment in time," Jack explained. "It contains information about the planet, as you knew and saw it. We won't find anything above the clouds because you didn't know there was anything there."

I didn't immediately understand.

"Compare it to Jefferson's life," Jack said. "If you checked his memories, you'd find infinitely more than this. You would be able to journey the stars, because Jeff knew they were there."

I viewed the environment again, and details of my time here started trickling back. I remembered when Kufe and I lived here... and then involuntarily, I recalled the day she had been taken away. I could hear echoes of myself weeping. I also knew that Kufe and I had been teenagers at the time of the incident – which clarified why I'd taken it so badly.

Curious, I turned to Kufe now. I'd never felt 'attracted' to her – as I had been to Sam – and I certainly wasn't considering it now. Still, Kufe was my partner; a fact I had accepted a while ago. She had demonstrated a commitment to helping me 'recover' – even before I knew I was recovering from anything. And although I'd initially proven difficult, she never gave up on me. Wasn't that what a *real* partner was?

Besides, she'd woven the most awesome landscape I'd ever seen... *just for me*. You can't beat that.

Kufe was staring into the distance. Certainly, I cherished her assistance thus far – but if she announced a desire to leave me, I would adapt myself accordingly. I realized I didn't feel any attachment to her, as I once must have. She turned to me and smiled, and I took her hand. My lessons on this prehistoric world were completed: there was no reason to stick around any longer. With a nod to Jack, we returned once more to the sunny landscape of Kufe's gift.

"I like it here," I told Jack.

"Don't blame you," he grinned. In all this time, he'd never left his chair. Kufe and I still sat by his feet.

Some time had passed, but I was no less energetic. I couldn't get over the fact that this place felt so *familiar* – almost as much as Jefferson's life still did.

"Why was this memory the clearest?" I asked.

"It was the most traumatizing for you," Jack replied. "As you saw, you were very young when her life was taken away. You took a life, and you got reprimanded for the first time in your existence.

Suffice it to say, you *never* killed after that."

I'd never enjoyed being corrected. The only trouble I had with authority is that I was scared of it – like I had been when I first saw the Tremendous Being. Knowing what I knew now, I couldn't help comparing the Council to my more-recent judge. The latter was now seen for the caricature it was; even the Collective outshone the Tremendous Being, and from what I heard, the Council was 'higher' than the Collective!

Speaking of which; I'd forgotten to ask Kufe about the Collective. Isn't it odd how thoughts link together like that? Jefferson Hurley always found that peculiar.

"Hey," I nudged Kufe. "Collective."

"Ooh, right," she said, and leaned against me. "Well, I knew many weavers that are now a part of it."

This explained why the Collective had greeted her so warmly. However, you can appreciate the difficulty of imagining three of your friends from three different parts of the world as one person – *literally*. It took me a moment to understand.

"Why didn't you merge with them… *it*?" I asked Kufe.

"You weren't there," she replied simply.

"But we were separated in the first place," I argued.

"Because *you* chose it," she smiled. I stared, puzzled.

"We are partners in a dance," she said. "From the moment the music began, we have been dancing." She hopped to her feet and began an elaborate, twirling dance around me. Jack rhythmically waved his hands, and a soft music began to play. Kufe's hypnotic movement continued for some time, and then ended as abruptly as it had started.

"Our dance is a complex one," she continued. "Sometimes, we can end our dance with different partners. It's okay, because we're all here to learn how to dance, anyway."

"What does that have to do with anything?" I asked.

"I chose to end my dance with you," she said, "Regardless of where and how we learn how to dance."

Her metaphor was clear enough. I fell silent, and marveled at her dedication. I swore to repay her at the first opportunity – although I hadn't the foggiest idea what form that opportunity or repayment would take. I looked up at Jack; he smiled at me and turned to look at the mountains.

Jack

I'm sure my conversation with Kufe triggered the next 'flashback.' Without warning, our surroundings were replaced by the hall of records from my second memory.

"I expected that," Jack said, exhaling a cloud of smoke. He was still staring where the Blue Mountains had been.

"I'm sure there's a 'No Smoking' sign here, somewhere," I said.

"Are you going to kick me out?" Jack challenged. I smiled and rose to my feet.

"Another reconstruction?" I asked Kufe, and pulled her up.

"Of course," she replied.

"I think I understand why," I said.

Around me, I noticed details I had previously missed. The pillars were segmented, and each had twelve equidistant vertical pinstripes of light. On the floor, wider strips of light ran through the base of each pillar, presumably their power source.

"Do you remember how these work?" Kufe asked, gesturing at the pillars. When I shook my head, she walked over to one and touched it. As I watched, each segment on the pillar rotated at varying degrees, and in varying directions. When they all settled, the pillar once again appeared to have unbroken pinstripes running down its length.

"As it looks," Kufe said, "It can store a lot of information."

She made the columns rotate again.

"When you do this, the pillar's form is changed. You have a new database, where you can store more information."

There isn't even a word for that number in English. I marveled at the technology that must have gone into constructing this place.

"This race later found more effective ways of storing information," Kufe continued. "At this time, the actual hall has been abandoned."

I was surprised. But I was also remembering something else; I looked up at the immense ceiling, and willed myself to rise above it. In moments, I stood atop the hall itself. The sight that awaited me triggered more memories of this life.

This place had been known as "Watchers of Perfection," because it occupied several moons of a large ringed planet (like Saturn). 'Perfection' was a reference to a sphere passing through a circle – the planet in its ring – regarded as a symbol of perfection by this civilization. Indeed, it would not be too far-fetched to say that some actually worshiped the planet.

What I called 'the hall of Records' was one of three large geodesic structures on one of the planet's moons. Similar gargantuan facilities and cities adorned most of the other satellites.

Standing atop the dome of the hall, I observed the other geodesic structures; one also for storage, and was linked to the main hall by a glass tunnel. The third housed our aircraft. It all returned so clearly. Kufe remembered it too.

"We did this," she said. "We stood here, that day."

"We did what?" I asked.

"The day you saw," she said, referring to the original memory. "After you remembered me, we came out here."

I recalled the day itself. I had very thankful to have my companion back. I realized now that I *loved* Kufe, but not in a way you're entirely familiar with. My affection for her covered every affectionate bond that can be shared on Earth; from vaguely affiliated coworkers to devoted siblings. I knew now that I could love her 'with the fire of a thousand stars' – a bit of poetry for you – but I could still cheer for her if she chose a path that excluded me. Needless to say, I was grateful that she intended to include me in her subsequent experiences.

My lesson was learned. I was glad that the bit about the priest was over as well. The avian had said that the priest was the drunk driver, hadn't he?

Something struck me. When 'it' did, my surroundings changed again without warning. This time, I was left standing in Jefferson's empty apartment.

Jack

9

Jack was nowhere in sight.

With some relief, I discovered Kufe was still with me. This was just another reconstruction. It caught me off guard, though; for a moment, I thought I *had* been dreaming, after all.

Broken sunbeams streamed through the window blinds. Even my old cell phone was on the floor. What little furniture I previously had was gone; I realized that this reconstruction was based on the eve of my death. It felt very *vacant*, like a stage after a play.

I was the only person in the building – probably in the entire world, if I ventured into it. But this was Jefferson Hurley's life, wasn't it? I smiled to think that it didn't feel so personal, anymore. I knew it was as real as the other two lives I had viewed. But what was the connection between this and those?

That was what had struck me. I hurried out the door, and Kufe followed.

Outside the building, a red pickup truck was parked at the stop sign. The engine wasn't running, and Jack sat on its hood, still smoking his unlit pipe.

"*You* were behind it, weren't you?"

"It worked, didn't it?" he chuckled. I stared at him for some time, and then grinned.

I couldn't help it.

"Thanks," I told him.

As Jack previously explained, the first Council was the first embodiment of the field of knowledge. Its presence had been necessary because the new 'sparks of consciousness' needed guidance. When arguments arose, an objective mediator was required; who better than the field of knowledge, which *stored* each side's argument *and* evidence?

You're probably wondering how a nonexistent entity can interact with people. There's no proof for its existence, is there? Besides, how can an immaterial thing represent itself as different individuals? Well, as Jack said – and *he* should know – anything is possible. I'll tell you more about this later.

Avatars like Jack represented the Council. The avian too was an avatar – but an older 'version' than Jack. Both were friends and mentors to Kufe and I, and had been so for thousands of years. Both were also directly responsible for finding the priest, and linking Jefferson to him. In doing so, the debt was repaid; my involvement with the priest was ended.

Kufe was watching me, her excitement perfectly concealed. She knew my memory was returning; she had known, all this time. I only now understood why she'd chosen to let me remember it on my own. I took her hand – this time in gratitude – and turned to Jack.

"My job here is done," he smiled, and got off the truck. His impressive robe changed to an old checkered suit, and his umbrella reappeared.

"See you around?" I asked him.

"Never too far away," he replied, and walked down the street, in the direction the truck had come from that night. A few steps down the road, he unfurled his umbrella and faded from sight.

Jack

10

"So that's it?" I said, turning to Kufe.

"That's it," she agreed.

Jeff's small town disappeared, and we hovered once more amidst the stars. They were even more awe-inspiring, now that I had seen so much. Kufe took my hand and we silently enjoyed the view.

My memory had returned. I even remembered the events that had taken place *before* I was born as Jefferson. That reminded me of something else. Kufe and I reappeared by the 'female' star.

"Welcome!" she greeted us. Kufe hugged her.

"I have a request," I told her. "I know you didn't answer my wishes as a child – but this one won't be hard."

"Name it," the star replied.

"Prevent me from ever returning to the Jewel," I said. "Just remind me about this trip."

She understood that my memory had returned, and lit up.

"Welcome back!" she greeted.

So, here's the other part you need to know.

I had been advised by the avian to consider spending some time on Earth. I was excited by the prospect; I saw the potential Earth has, and I was eager to bring some things I'd learned at the Cycle of Perfection. I'd been to Earth before, and for some reason, I was looking forward to doing it again. Both Kufe and the star had been aware of my plans, and they had eagerly encouraged me.

I would have once concluded by saying that going to Earth was a bad idea. Now, I know that it happened because it had to. Still, I wasn't looking to repeat the trip any time soon.

I only hoped the 'priest' – the truck driver – was okay, and that he didn't get judged too harshly.

As I watched Kufe conversing with the star, I decided she had been right, earlier. *This* was home; I had some catching up to do with my family.

But you're still wondering about the third memory, aren't you? The one with the words.

Appropriately, it was my last flashback, occurring sometime after Kufe and I returned to the star. As Kufe conversed with the star, I remembered how Jefferson hadn't even been aware of their existence. Yet here I was, loved and loving them as if I had never left. My friends had never called on 'Jefferson' – who didn't even believe in the paranormal – because they knew that I would be back.

As thoughts drifted through my mind, I recalled the third memory. I know now that I *am* the one who wanders through all. You are wandering within the same Universe. Our stories never end, and we always add a new chapter – a new *thread* – to the tales we weave.

That's it; that's my story – or as I said, the important bits.

Now, there is something I must attend to. Before I do, I'd like to show you one last thing. Perhaps we can finish our conversation along the way.

We, the wanderers

You know, dying' was once a respected thing. In preparing for the transition, some cultures arranged to have someone calm the dying through the process. This reverence was later replaced by fear, and any talk of death was labeled as *morbid*. Perhaps, armed with such knowledge, Jefferson wouldn't have fought death as vehemently as he did. But as you remember, he brought his fear out of the Jewel – your Earth – with him.

Like I said before, I have no regrets. Given the opportunity to change Jefferson's life, I wouldn't touch anything. His fear of death made my subsequent experiences more meaningful. I have learned many valuable lessons thus far, and I'm sure there are yet more to be found.

Still, these have been *my* experiences. I can't blame you for finding them a little far-fetched. I won't try to convince you, though; some things are best seen in person. You will also remember things when you are adequately prepared.

I'll be avoiding Earth for some time, like I said. Maybe two to three thousand years. After that, I may drop by for a visit. If you're around, I'll look you up.

***

Well, we're here.

Yes, it's my library. I neglected to mention something else; this is where I come to rejuvenate, after every life. I built it because I considered it a preferable alternative to going to The City. It's like taking a hot shower at the end of a sweaty workday; certainly preferable to cleaning up in a public bathroom.

Now, don't get me wrong. The City is infinitely cleaner and far more sophisticated than anything on Earth. However, I like the quiet simplicity this place provides. Besides, I get to spend quality time with my avian friend. You can join us in conversation, sometime; I'm sure it would be enjoyable.

I brought you here to satisfy your curiosity. Like Jefferson, you probably want to see the inside. There's no point in showing you, but there's no point in hiding it either.

Looks a bit bland, doesn't it? You'd think that there would be more to a pyramid this size than a bare twelve square-foot room. The design is deliberate. I have lived many lives in spartan conditions, and I must admit I've developed a taste for it. Still, this is no ordinary bare room. See how the walls come alive with energy? When I command it, they will generate a small field of light, in which I shall 'bathe' and store my memories. To briefly explain it, I'll be reviewing memories from my beginnings, so I can clearly see Jefferson's life in context.

Sadly, I must leave you at this time. I have to rest; afterwards, I plan to seek my avian friend. When I have spoken to him, I will find you. But this may take some time. As you recall, there are two star gates on either side of this pyramid. You may use the left one to return home, when you're ready. The other one will take you to The City. And whether or not you have believed me, remember the things I told you.

I'll see you around.

Fin

The Author

Raphael Okure was born and raised in Nigeria, long after dinosaurs had roamed the Earth. He later moved to the United States, where he developed an appetite for fast food and a curiosity about extraterrestrial intelligence. While he doesn't personally know any aliens, he would like to use this medium to invite them for a cup of tea.

Raphael has several High School Diplomas (it's true; I've seen them), a Certificate in Fine Arts and Design, and an unnamed degree from the University of Life, where he currently studies and lectures. Raphael is also a full-time father to a vivacious young guitar.

Other tools for peace from Peace Evolutions, LLC:

Peace and Forgiveness
by Jefferson Glassie
ISBN 0-9753837-0-1, 112 pages, $14.95
This life is our perfection, says the author. Who could imagine any heaven more perfect than this earth, with butterflies, snowflakes, and mountain tops? Though we are all peace and love, man has fears that cause war, anger, hate, and everything that isn't love. Letting go of fear – forgiving - brings peace. If we learn this, we can change the world.

Also available:
Double Audio CD read by the author
ISBN 0-9753837-1-X, $14.95

Poems of Peace and Forgiveness
by Jefferson Glassie
ISBN 0-9753837-2-8, 72 pages, $12.95
With photographs by the author
This book captures the concepts from Glassie's book, Peace and Forgiveness. These beautiful poems explain there's no right or wrong, no evil or sin, in the Universe. Everything that's not love is just based on fear. Glassie teaches the lessons of forgiveness that can lead to peace of mind, and peace in our society. We are all one, in perfection.

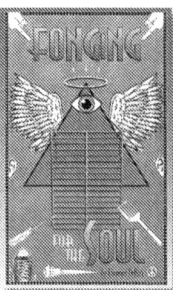

Fonging for the Soul
by Erasmus Caffery
ISBN 0-9753837-3-6, 78 pages, $14.95
Gathering with others, tapping on an oven rack attached to strings tied to fingers that are stuck in your ears, listening to primal sounds. Fonging brings us to together in laughter, and is much more sane than war. This book explains how
to fong. It's very simple and you can do it with anyone.
By understanding the simultaneous silliness and splendor of life, we learn to create a better and more peaceful world through inanity. With many helpful illustrations, because you'll need them.

Songs of Peace and Forgiveness
ISBN 0-9753837-4-4, $16.98
Featuring original and public domain songs by Gaye Adegbalola, Scott Ainslie, Roddy Barnes, Eleanor Ellis (on a Bill Ellis song), Andra Faye and the Mighty Good Men, Grant Dermody and Frank Fotusky, Allen Holmes and Alison Radcliffe, Kelley Hunt (on a Jim Ritchey song),
Ray Kaminsky, Mark Kinniburgh, MSG – The Acoustic Blues Trio, Jesse Palidofsky, and Alex Radus. The most unique blues CD you've ever heard. It will make your heart soar. Proceeds go to help preserve the famous "Barbershop" in Washington, DC run by the Archie Edwards Blues Heritage Foundation, winner of The Blues Foundation's 2005 Keeping The Blues Alive (KBA) Award.

My Love Affair with an Island: The History of the Jefferson Islands Club and St. Catherine's Island
by Jefferson Glassie
ISBN 0-9753837-5-2, 128 pages, $20
With photographs
This book tells the history of the famous Jefferson Islands Club, called the "Playground of Presidents," which was the private island retreat for Presidents including Franklin Roosevelt and Harry Truman as well as many Senators and Congressmen. With many humorous anecdotes and comments, Glassie recounts the history of both Poplar Islands where the Club was initially located and St. Catherine's Island, mixing in tales of politicians and watermen, along with the harm caused by erosion and the gradual degradation of the health of the Bay.

Rest in the Knowing
By Lynda Allen
ISBN 0-9753837-6-0, 98 pages, $15
With photographs
"Rest in the Knowing, is broken down into seven groups of four outstanding poems each. The poems reflect every person s journey of life that is NOT a straight path going from darkness to light. It is a path that often veers wildly back from one to the other but with each leg of the journey a feeling of being closer to the truth. Few people are able to express with such eloquence the inner feelings, and desires every human experiences." Christopher Ian Chenoweth, Publisher, Daily Inspiration.

ORDER FORM

Fax orders to (301) 263-9280 with completed order form.
Email orders by logging on to www.peace-evolutions.com
Telephone orders by calling (301) 263-9282.
Postal orders may be sent to: **Peace Evolutions, LLC**
P.O. Box 458-31, Glen Echo, MD 20812-0458

Please send the following:

Peace and Forgiveness, book	$14.95 each	quantity: _____
Peace and Forgiveness, audio CD	$14.95 each	quantity: _____
Poems of Peace and Forgiveness, book	$12.95 each	quantity: _____
Songs of Peace and Forgiveness, CD	$16.98 each	quantity: _____
Fonging for the Soul	$14.95 each	quantity: _____
My Love Affair With An Island	$20.00 each	quantity: _____
Rest in the Knowing	$15.00 each	quantity: _____
Spirit Wanderer	$15.00 each	quantity: _____

We will honor all requests for full refund on returned items.

Please send more free information on:
❏ presentations   ❏ other publications and information

Name:_____

Address: _____

City: _____ State:_____ Zip: _____

Telephone: _____

Email address: _____

Sales tax: Please add 5.00% for products shipped to Maryland addresses.

Shipping and handling:
United States: $5.00 for first book/CD and $2.00 for each additional item.
International: $7.00 for first book and $5.00 for each additional item.

Payment:
❏ Check   or   Credit Card
❏ Visa   ❏ Master Card

Card number: _____ Exp. Date:_____

Name on Card: _____

www.ingramcontent.com/pod-product-compliance
Lightning Source LLC
LaVergne TN
LVHW011711060526
838200LV00051B/2856